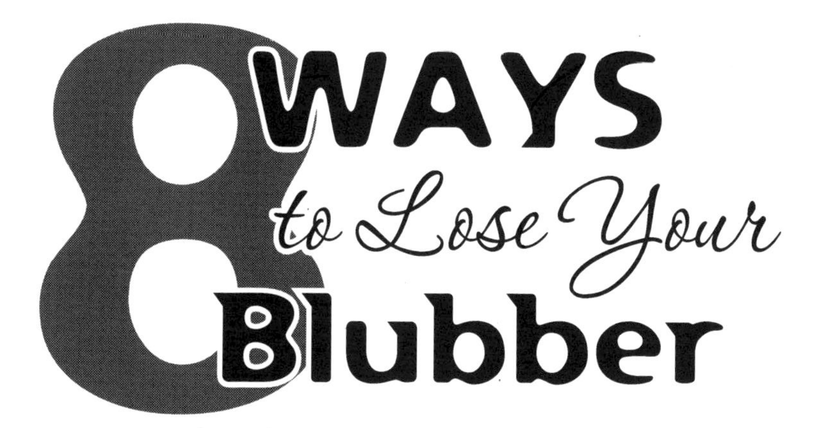


**Through Hormone Balancing and Lifestyle Changes**

*An easy-to-use guide to help you understand how hormones and food affect everything!*

If you are having trouble losing weight or body fat, you may need to explore one or all of these ways to lose your blubber. For some it may be only diet and exercise, but for most it will be a variety of dietary and lifestyle changes and hormone balancing.

ISBN: 1451536690
ISBN-13: 9781451536690

# Dedication

I dedicate this book to all men, women, and children who have struggled with weight, mood, and health challenges. I am truly grateful for the thousands of people who have trusted me with their darkest emotional, medical, and eating secrets. They have openly cried, laughed, and shared very private information that enabled me to assess their needs and put them on the road to healing.

I am especially grateful to my two sons, Preston and Dillon, for their love and inspiration, which keep my soul nourished. I appreciate all my family for unconditionally loving me.

I want to thank my best friend Kathleen Stefancin, for supporting me in writing this book and for her constant kindness. Thank you to all whom I have not mentioned—for being eternally patient with me and my long working hours. With your love and friendship all my efforts have been worthwhile and rewarding. I'm grateful for you all and cherish each and every one of your individual spirits!

# Table of Contents

# Introduction

I have always had a great intuitive, positive passion for life, supported by a warmhearted and fun-loving family. My personal journey and interest in achieving good health started when I was about ten years old, many years before I thought about becoming a dietitian. I had been at a family party and overheard several relatives talking about one of my aunts' illness. I felt very sad about the situation and knew, then, I wanted to help people with their health and make sure I had a healthy future. I remember thinking, "I can be different, even with 'bad' genes." At that time, I didn't know my vision was similar to the concept of nutrigenomics—the use of food and supplements to change a person's genetic code for health.

To my surprise, many years later I found myself faced with similar challenges and learned I had inherited obesity and disease genes from both sides of my family. In fact, I grew up with several obese family members experiencing a variety of medical issues.

I decided to become a dietitian to learn how food could play a role in health. So, how did I get involved with studying hormones and supplements if learning about food was my primary interest? In 2002, I became the clinical director of an integrative compounding pharmacy. In addition to investigating quality supplements, the pharmacist asked me to put together a program for assessing men and women's hormones.

If you would have told me that my future in nutrition would lead to counseling clients about hormones, I would have said, "You're crazy! I'm not that old." But after listening carefully to so many of my patients who were suffering for years without relief from their symptoms, and athletes with weight fluctuations, I was forced to look deeper into the underlying problems and not just treat the symptoms, especially since so many of my patients had seen so many health practitioners before they stepped into my office. In addition to looking at diet and lifestyle, I began to think about how hormones play a role in health.

Three complaints stood out most with my patients: "I'm tired," "I'm depressed," and "I want to lose weight." In the past, these patients were given prescription drugs for these symptoms without questioning them deeper to uncover what may be causing the problems. Many of them reported trying a variety of medications for anxiety, depression, and other hormonal issues, but they continued to experience a downward spiral of erratic menstrual periods, anger, sleep disturbances, worsened fatigue, depression, and weight gain. Traditional therapy for many women with these symptoms involved a birth control pill, then an antidepressant, then an anti anxiety medication, and then a sleep aid. But new symptoms continued to manifest and they ended up in my office.

I'm sure many of you can relate to this scenario or know someone in a similar situation. These cycles of medical symptoms can last for three months to 10 years or even forever. Unfortunately, these cycles leave you feeling fatter, angrier, more depressed, and tired. Both men and women going through these challenges report feeling emotionally flat, no libido, more tired, even after exercise, and a poor sense of well-being, often stating, "I do not feel like myself."

All this can be changed if you obtain the right subjective and objective assessments. You need to become an advocate of your own health and well-being. There are many dietary factors you can assess on your own to facilitate your healing process that will be talked about in this book. Other assessments may require blood work and evaluation by your health practitioner. An integrative approach could help in resolving your symptoms. This may involve some forms of whole food, herbal, vitamin, mineral, homeopathic, synthetic hormonal replacement support (HRT), or bio-identical hormonal (BHRT) support, as well as stress reduction techniques.

I have learned through years of counseling and personal health struggles that there are eight ways to dig deeper into the issues around losing your blubber and regaining your sanity. Some involve food, diet, and exercise, and others involve your hormones. Together these eight parameters will give you the secrets to losing weight and body fat. If one of these ways is out of balance, often you will have a hard time losing weight and body fat. Lifestyle changes and balancing your hormones are the answers to losing weight and body fat permanently.

The purpose of this book is to help you begin this individualized healing process. I have used the techniques and guidelines in this book with my patients for over fifteen years and have found them to be effective in relieving their symptoms, encouraging weight and body fat loss, and giving them their life back. I will provide you with easy-to-use calculations, optimal health ideas, and specific supplement recommendations. You will also learn about specific tests that you can request from your health practitioner. The information in this book will empower you with the right questions and answers to your struggles with weight loss and feeling good.

The bottom line is that we are given one body and mind in this lifetime. The good news is that, at a cellular level, you can have a new body and mind in about twelve months. The healing begins with your commitment to long-term nutritional changes and balancing your hormones. My sincere intention is that this book will inspire you and lead you down the right path to achieving your ideal body, your dreams, and an extraordinary quality of life. *Eight Ways to Lose Your Blubber* is more than just teaching you how to lose body fat and weight loss. It's about overall quality of life and joy. It's about empowering you with tools that will change your life. The only way you can fail is to give up! Please don't do that!

The key to good health is not fad diets, exercise apparatuses, pills, or super foods. The solution is individualizing your calories, carbohydrate-protein-fat ratios, activity level, the right supplement intake, and, if needed, balancing hormones.

I wish you the best of health and happiness. LIVE! Be present! Namaste.

# CHAPTER ONE: Calorie and Food Monitoring

The first chapter may seem like obvious steps that most people know about but do not follow. What are calories and why do they matter? A calorie is a unit that measures energy, sort of like the watts on a light bulb. It takes more energy (watts) to burn a brighter bulb, just as it takes more energy (calories) to climb the stairs than to use the elevator. If you eat more than you use, then you will gain weight and body fat. This occurs whether the extra calories come from too big a meal or spread out over the course of a day.

All calories count. They count during good times like vacations and birthdays, and they count during stressful times like a new date, a funeral, or a business meeting. Many of my patients report overeating during the good times and the stressful times. For example, during a stressful business meeting, one patient reported drinking two or three glasses of wine and three pieces of bread in addition to lunch. Pay attention to when you find yourself eating more than usual. Taking in too many calories will result in weight gain.

Calories seem to count even more after the age of twenty-five. This is because after age twenty-five, you lose more than half a pound of muscle per year, which increases your body fat and often weight gain. The good news is that you have a choice. You can maintain your weight and even gain muscle mass as you age if you eat a low-fat diet primarily consisting of plant foods and lean protein and continue strength training.

The number one problem I see with patients regarding calories is that they do not spread out their meals throughout the day properly. If they did, their body would use the calories from those meals and not store them as fat. We all know people who go on a weight-loss program for months and lose weight the first two to eight weeks but then hit a plateau with their weight loss. The problem is that the weight loss is mostly water and muscle and not body fat. This is because they often skip breakfast or eat a tiny 60-180-calorie meal such as a granola bar, followed by a tiny lunch, snack, or dessert, then go through the afternoon without adequate fluids or food. They come home feeling ravenous and proceed to binge on a variety of junk food, pizza, snacks, ice cream, candy, alcohol, or just overeat at dinner. The rest of the evening is spent in a stupor, never feeling relaxed or satisfied because the calories in their meals were not spread out properly throughout the day.

So how many calories do we need to eat every day? Based on the thousands of women and men I have counseled, I have found most women generally need between 1,200 and 2,000 calories per day, and most men need between 1,500 and 2,500 calories per day. Keep in mind that these calorie levels depend on how much body fat you have, your activity level, height, weight, genetics, and even how much sleep you get each night.

There are three easy ways to calculate your calorie needs without consulting a health or exercise professional.

**1) Take your weight and add a zero.** **For example: I weigh 140 pounds. Add a zero and that equals 1,400 calories. I need approximately 1,400 calories without a lot of exercise to maintain my current weight of 140 pounds.

**2) Use a handheld device or scale method** (both are bioelectric impedance analysis methods). These methods will assess your body fat percentage. Use the percentage to calculate your calories. Multiply your percentage of body fat by your weight to find your pounds of fat. Then, to find your pounds of lean muscle mass, subtract your pounds of fat from your weight. Move the decimal over one place to the right to get the estimated amount of daily calories needed per day with low activity. If you exercise for thirty minutes three times per week or walk around at your job (do not sit at a desk), then multiply the daily calories you found by 1.3 to get your final daily needed calories.

**For example:**

My body fat is 18.0%, and my weight is 140 pounds (140 x 0.18 = 25.2 pounds of fat).
140 pounds - 25.2 pounds of fat = 114.8 pounds of lean mass
To 114.8 pounds of lean mass, add a zero = 1,148 calories/day
1,148 calories x 1.3 moderate activity = 1,492 calories/day needed

To lose body fat you have to eat 500 fewer calories per day for a week or burn an extra 500 calories per day through exercise.

If you want to gain weight, you must consume 500 calories more than your body's needs per day. If this calculation method doesn't result in your desired weight loss or weight gain, depending on your personal goals, the third way of determining calorie needs may be more accurate for your body type.

**3) Keep track of your daily calories and food portions by keeping a food diary.** There are two kinds of food diaries: a handwritten food diary and a computer analysis program. Tracking your food intake with a written food diary is one of the most helpful and practical methods you can use to maintain your weight. It is imperative that you write down the foods right before or after you eat to be accurate. Our memories are not always as sharp as we think. For example, one of my patients recorded everything she ate and drank and tracked her steps with a pedometer. She was not losing weight and she was eating within the calorie range we calculated by using methods one and two, but after we tracked her calories through her food diary plus her activity level; we found that she actually needed fewer calories to lose body fat.

The food diary allows you see exactly what you are eating and keeps you honest and on track. By recording exactly what you eat, how much you eat, and the time you eat, you can gauge how much you eat at each meal, and how many calories you have left for the day. An even better proactive approach is to write down ahead of time what you plan to eat for your next meal or that whole day. I recommend eating at least every three to four hours. That way you will be getting the necessary four to six mini meals and healthy snacks per day. I am a single mom with two boys ages twelve and fourteen and work full time. I am a very busy woman and have found tracking calories and activity works the best for most people. It also makes you accountable.

The other food diary involves a computer analysis program. There are many great programs that you can use as a food diary, but they have three drawbacks: 1) they take time, 2) they are not practical (are you going track your foods the rest of your life?), and 3) people fill out their food diary online at the end of the day, missing many snacks and foods they ate throughout the day. For the highly technical person or a professional athlete, these computer programs can be very helpful and precise. Do not use or buy a program with all the bells and whistles that you will not use!

### Calculating calories, carbohydrates, and proteins, fat in your handwritten food diary

Most people who lose weight gain it back within two years after their "diet," often with a few extra, unwanted pounds. It can be very difficult to keep a food diary long term. If you learn these practical guidelines you will be able to go out to eat, travel, work, and *live* while maintaining your weight goals with or without a food diary.

1) If a food has a nutrition label, read it. Do not guess. Be sure to understand the serving size. It may be half the bag, 1 slice, 1 ounce, 12 pieces, etc. This is the most important rule, and it includes milk and yogurt.

2) If you plan to eat out, Google the restaurant first to see if it has a nutrition facts page. Choose a smaller size, eat an appetizer for a meal, share a meal, or bring half home to eat for a meal next day.
3) In all other cases, memorize these general exchange facts that I use and find to be practical and most accurate:

**Most grain carbohydrates**: ½ cup of rice, pasta, or cereal; 1 slice of bread; ½ regular size bagel; and ¼ cup of quinoa all equal approximately 15 grams of carbohydrates and about 80 calories.

**Fruit carbohydrates**: ½ cup of fruit; 1 small piece of whole fruit; ½ banana; or about 1 cup of any kind of berry all equal approximately 15 grams of carbohydrates and about 60 calories.

**Sugar**: make sure most packaged foods and bars contain 6 grams of sugar per serving or less. Fresh fruit doesn't count in this rule.

**Protein**: 1 ounce of any lean meat (loin, flank, round, or filet cuts), poultry, tuna, or seafood; 1 whole organic egg; or 2 egg whites all equal approximately 7 grams of protein and about 35-75 calories.

**Fats**: 1 teaspoon of any kind (butter or oil) both equals approximately 5 grams of fat and about 45 calories.

Review question: how would you evaluate the protein, carbohydrates, and fat in crackers, M&M'S, milk, cheese, or yogurt per serving? Remember, these foods have nutrition fact labels.

Here are a few shocking calorie facts so you will understand why it's important to read food labels and plan ahead when eating out. I am not saying that you can't ever eat these foods, but if you can't lose weight, this information could be a rude awakening, and you may want to choose other foods.

**Two Subway cookies with your lower-calorie sandwich and water add 420 calories.

**Average "fancy" six-inch diameter bagel has approximately 350 calories or more.

**Name-brand real ice creams can contain 360 or more calories per ½ cup.

**One "Bloomin' Onion" from Outback Steakhouse has over 2,000 calories and over 100 grams of fat.

Keep in mind these food choice guidelines when selecting healthier foods. Start by eating more whole, raw, unprocessed organic foods. This means fruits, vegetables, nuts and seeds, organic free range eggs, lean organic protein, or wild fish such as salmon. Avoid frozen, boxed, canned, and fast foods as much as possible.

## Food Monitoring

Let's look at how food monitoring plays a role in weight. Food monitoring can help you assess your calories, food portions, and meal timing, and see eating patterns that aren't in your best interests to lose weight. Depending on your personal goal, food monitoring can help you maintain your weight and lose body fat, lose weight and body fat, or gain weight.

Here are some easy tips to follow if you want to maintain or lose weight.

1) Don't eat after 7 p.m.
2) Eat at home as much as you can, or pack a lunch or snack as often as possible.
3) Don't skip meals—consuming inadequate calories stresses the body and often leads to eating binges.

The following tips can be very helpful if you want to gain weight. They are my top three recommendations for weight gain, and they work every time when adjusted to meet your body's caloric needs.

1) Eat lean protein in the evening with a healthy carbohydrate. Try 4-6 organic egg whites or ¼-½ cup of Egg Beaters, a whey or plant-based shake (such as Complete Shake, made by NSA), and a carbohydrate like a pear.
2) Add nutrient-dense foods that contain lots of calories with low volume so you aren't as overly full. Some examples of high-calorie, low-volume foods are ¼ to ½ cup of any nuts or seeds added to a salad or eaten with an apple at snack time.
3) Add healthy fats to your meals or snacks. Add 1 teaspoon-2 tablespoons of flax oil with lignans, olive oil, or coconut oil to your cooking, salads, shakes, or foods.

**Summary:**

Eating too little or too many calories at meals can contribute to weight gain and increased body fat. Start with a specific calorie or habit change. If it doesn't work, monitor your food intake with a food journal, adjust your food intake or activity level, eat at least four to six mini meals per day and seek a health professional to assess other possible causes of your lack of progress.

# CHAPTER TWO: Carbohydrate, Protein, and Fat Ratios

It's a myth that all calories are equal. What if you have followed all the advice listed in chapter one (followed a calorie-restricted program, kept a food diary, ate at least four to six mini meals a day) but you stopped losing weight or still have a sugar or carbohydrate craving resulting in overeating intermittently or even bingeing on junk food like a bag of M&M'S? You may need to balance or alter your carbohydrate, protein, and fat ratios. Your metabolic rate depends on the thermic effect of food. Thermogenic means how fast you burn calories (expend energy). Fat is the least thermogenic (it burns calories slower), carbohydrates are next, and protein is the most thermogenic. Therefore, sometimes people are heavier than they wish because of eating too much food high in fat or carbohydrates.

The following guidelines have helped most of my clients stay within the appropriate grams and ratios of carbohydrate, protein, and fat (ideal nutrients) to maintain their weight and body fat goals:

Carbohydrates: 30%-50% of daily calories
Protein: 10%-30% of daily calories
Fat: 15%-30% of daily calories

It is important to keep in mind that these guidelines have been appropriate for about 75% of my clients, typically between the ages of thirty-five and sixty, who exercise moderately (three to four times per week for thirty to sixty minutes each time). We should always consider individualizing all recommendations. Every body is different.

Here is an example of how these guidelines do not fit for a close friend of mine. She is a raw-food advocate who eats at least 80% of her calories as carbohydrates and is thinner and healthier than most women over fifty. Can I eat 80% carbohydrates, feel good, and keep a healthy weight? No way! Even when I train for a marathon, I have to keep my carbohydrate around 50%-55% of my total calories .This is probably because I come from an obese family and I have a hard time processing a higher percent of carbohydrates, even when I am doing endurance events. Remember, each body has different needs!

First keep a food diary, and then, if you are not having progress with your body fat loss, use the guidelines below to calculate how many grams you need of each nutrient based on your weight goals and caloric needs. This has helped many of my patients lose that extra 10 pounds and feel good!

**Ideal Nutrients**

**Ideal Protein:**
Minimum Recommended Dietary Allowance (RDA): 0.8 grams/kg (kilogram)

1 pound = 2.2 kg
Example: 150-pound (68 kg) person needs 54 grams/day of protein
Example: 200-pound (91 kg) person needs 73 grams/day of protein
(To get 54 grams of protein, take 150 pounds, divide it by 2.2 kg/pound = 68 kg. This gives you your kilograms [kg] of body weight. Then take 68 kg x 0.8 g/kg = 54 grams of protein.)

****Remember you are eating a higher protein intake because it is the most metabolically active nutrient, meaning you burn protein calories the easist.**

Weight loss: 1.0-1.4 g/kg, and up to no more than 1 gram/pound
Example: 150 pounds (68 kg): 68-95-150 g/day
Example: 200 pounds (91 kg): 91-127-200 g/day

Athletes: 1.2-1.6 g/kg
Example: 150 pounds (68 kg): 82-109 g/day
Example: 200 pounds (91 kg): 109-146 g/day

**Ideal Carbohydrates:**

Fast body fat loss: less than 130 g/day
Weight loss, with activity less than three hours a week: 130-200 g/day

Average person: 4-5 g/kg/day
Example: 150 pounds (68 kg): 272-340 g/day
Example: 200 pounds (91 kg): 364-455 g/day

Athletes exercising one to three hours/day: 7-10 g/kg/day
Example: 150 pounds (68 kg): 476-680 g/day
Example: 200 pounds (91 kg): 637-910 g/day

Athletes exercising four or more hours/day: 12-13 g/kg
Example: 150 pounds (68 kg): 816-884 g/day
Example: 200 pounds (91 kg): 1,092-1,183 g/day

**Ideal Fat:**

Weight and body fat loss: 15%-25% of daily calories
Example: 25-42 g/day if you need 1,500 calories/day
Example: 33-56 g/day if you need 2,000 calories/day
(For example, if you need 2,000 calories per day, you would take 2,000 x 0.15 [15%] =300, divide by 9 calories/gram of fat = 33 grams of fat needed per day.)

If you are not trying to achieve body fat or weight loss, follow these general guidelines: 20%-30% of calories from fat
Example: 33-50 g/day if you need 1,500 calories/day
Example: 44-67 g/day if you need 2,000 calories/day

*Wow*, you've made it through the numbers! However, if you still find it difficult to understand what you need based on these calculations, I have provided the following meal, snack, and menu choices to make it even easier for you to be successful with your weight goals. This information pulls all that you have learned together from chapters one and two to lose body fat and reach your weight goals.

**Each meal should contain the following servings based on chapter one's general exchange facts. This**

**will balance your carbohydrate, protein, and fat intake:**

Approximately 2-3 servings of carbohydrates, 30-45 grams total
You can eat as many vegetables as desired, except starchy vegetables (peas, corn, yams, and potatoes, which count in your total carbohydrate grams)
3-8 ounces of lean protein (21-56 grams total)
1-3 fat servings (5-15 grams total)
**2:1 carbohydrate: protein ratio (30 grams of carbohydrates: 15 grams of protein)

**Each snack should contain:**

1-2 servings of carbohydrates (15-30 grams total)
1-4 ounces of protein (7-28 grams total)
Up to 1-2 fat servings (5-10 grams total)
**2:1 (carbohydrate: protein) ratio, but for body fat loss a 1:1 (carbohydrate: protein) ratio is better for snack time.

It is important to remember to eat carbohydrates, protein, and fats together at most meals and snacks. Most importantly, eat them in balance. For example, an ideal breakfast may consist of 1 slice of whole grain bread (15 grams of carbohydrates), ½ cup of fresh fruit (another 15 grams of carbohydrates), 1 whole organic egg (7 grams of protein) and 2 egg whites (7 more grams of protein) scrambled with fresh sautéed spinach using some cooking spray or a pan lightly coated in olive oil. This meal equals a total of 30 grams of carbohydrates to 14 grams of protein, about a 2:1 ratio for your first meal of the day. The fat is about 5-14 grams of fat (depending on oil choice). This is a well-balanced meal for weight loss using the 2:1 ratio of carbohydrates: protein intake.

Snacks are best eaten at a 1:1 carbohydrate: protein/fat ratio, or a 2:1 ratio. An example of a 1:1 ratio would be 2-6 whole grain crackers (15 grams of carbohydrates) and 1 ounce of tuna mixed with some fat-free cottage cheese for moisture). A lot of people experience an afternoon crash and grab a granola bar, pretzels, a piece of chocolate, a soda, an energy drink, or even a bag of cookies from the vending machine. These foods mainly provide carbohydrates without adequate protein and healthy fats. Another example of a good snack with a 2:1 ratio would be an apple and 2-4 tablespoons of almonds. This snack contains carbohydrates, protein, and healthy fats in the proper ratios, providing glucose stability and therefore helping with weight and body fat loss. Plus, you won't raid the refrigerator after work if you eat healthy snacks and meals every three to four hours during the day.

As an example, I have provided you with a sample two-day menu below. Keep in mind when choosing healthier foods as shown on this menu to buy organic when possible. Begin by eating more whole, raw, unprocessed foods, such as fresh fruits, vegetables, nuts, seeds. If you eat animal protein, choose lean meat, free range eggs, or wild fish such as salmon. These examples are choices that my patients have found to be easy and tasty, and they were able to lose weight without being overly hungry.

## Sample Menu

| Day | Breakfast 6-7 am | Snack 9-10 am | Lunch 12-1 pm | Snack 3-4 pm | Dinner 6-7:30 pm | Snack If very hungry |
|---|---|---|---|---|---|---|
| **Mon.** | ½ banana and ½ cup dry Kashi cereal with one free range organic whole egg and 3-4 egg whites or egg beaters. Water or green tea | ½ cup of fat free cottage cheese and ½-1 cup of fresh or frozen organic berries | 3 oz cooked chicken breast chopped and mixed with 3-4 grapes, onions and celery. Placed on whole grain bread. Carrot sticks on the side | Organic Apple string cheese | Sweet potato, 4 oz wild salmon, salad with many raw veggies added with vinegar and olive oil | Complete Shake or Whey Shake made with water or 8 oz water |
| **Tue.** | Complete Shake made with water, 1-2 Tbsp of ground flax meal and ½-1 cup of frozen fruit or if no fruit can use 8 oz of skim, soy, almond or rice milk | Protein Bar 200-300 calories- zero trans fat, less than 6 grams of sugar, 2:1 or 1:1 ratio of carb: protein | 1 cup of wild rice or brown rice, 3 oz of sautéed shrimp and with sautéed spinach | 1-2 oz of tuna, made with cottage cheese or low fat mayo on 4-6 whole grain crackers | 3 small boiled red potatoes, 3-4 oz filet and 1 cup of broc- coli and carrots | Egg whites with a sprinkle of parmesan cheese (and ½ cup of fruit or, mini bag of popcorn if necessary) |
| **Wed.** | ¼-½ dry cup oat- meal made with water, add ½ cup of blueber- ries and one slice of Canadian bacon on side | 2-4 Tbs nuts or seeds or 1/3 cup of soy nuts & 12 grapes | Whole wheat pita wrap with Turkey and veggies | 1 green smoothie/ blended salad | 1 cup of whole wheat pasta, 1 cup sautéed zucchini, mushrooms, tomatoes and onions in olive oil and tofu | 1 piece of fruit or cup of green tea with flavored Stevia |

In this chapter, I also wanted to talk about fiber since it is a carbohydrate. Let's make this topic easy. There are two kinds of fiber, insoluble (grains and lentils) and soluble (apples and flax seeds). We need a combination of both kinds of fiber. Most professional organizations agree that we need at least 25 to 35 grams of fiber per day. You can consume up to 50 grams a day, but I encourage a slow increase so bloating, gas, and excessive bowel movements don't stop you in your tracks! Fiber helps with regularity, a feeling of fullness (satiety), and insulin resistance, which we will be talking about in the next chapter.

The way to obtain adequate fiber if you don't have a gluten sensitivity is to start your day with whole grain cereal or a healthy shake that contains at least 10 to 14 grams of fiber per serving, zero trans fatty acids, and less than 6 grams of sugar. If you are too busy for breakfast, make a shake. NSA's Complete Shake, which is one of my favorite shakes, contains 4 grams of fiber and helps you on your way to reaching your goal of 25 to 35 grams of fiber per day. It's quick and easy, and by adding a little flax seed or fiber powder and ½-1 cup of mixed berries to the shake you can increase your fiber intake to 10-14 grams. This shake is also very nutrient dense, contains low to moderate calories: 110 per scoop, and will get you out the door feeling satisfied. Best of all, you've only consumed about 200 to 300 calories. You can also make a snack mix that includes whole grain cereal with some soy nuts or nuts and a sprinkling of dried fruit, just for flavoring, and then scoop 1 cup into a baggie or little container and eat it on the bus, train, or in your car on the way to school or class.

To sum up this chapter, I would like to share a case study of a patient who had a slightly elevated glucose level, struggled to lose 20 pounds weight and felt fatigued. In her case, I took a food history while simultaneously starting her on the following program to provide her with the correct calories, percentages, and grams of carbohydrates, protein, and fats to help her with energy while losing body fat.

She needed 1,600 calories per day based on her weight and activity level to lose weight. Her calories were distributed as follows: 50% carbohydrates, 20% protein and 30% fat. To figure the grams of each nutrient, you will need to know that each gram of carbohydrate has 4 calories, each gram of protein has 4 calories, and each gram of fat has 9 calories.

So, we can use the following calculations to figure out how many grams of each nutrient she needs:

Carbohydrates: 1,600 calories multiplied by 0.50 (50%) = 800 calories, divided by 4 calories/gram = 200 grams of carbohydrates per day

**Now to figure out the servings of daily carbohydrates: take 200 grams divided by 15 (grams/serving of carbohydrates) = 13 servings/day of fruit, bread, etc.

Protein: 1,600 calories multiplied by 0.20 (20%) = 320 calories, divided by 4 calories/gram = 80 grams of protein per day

**Now to figure out the servings of daily protein: take 80 grams divided by 7 (grams of protein per ounce of protein) = 11 ounces of lean protein/day.

Fat: 1,600 calories multiplied by 0.30 (30%) = 480 calories, divided by 9 calories/gram = 53 grams of fat per day

**Now to figure out the servings of daily fat: take 53 grams divided by 5 (5 grams of fat per 1 teaspoon) = 11 teaspoons/day

In more difficult cases, consult a registered dietitian, a nutrition-qualified health professional, or a certified personal trainer to help you figure out these numbers. I often change the carbohydrate:protein:fat ratios every two to eight weeks to help the body keep responding to weight and body fat loss. Some active people need a 3:1 carbohydrate ratio, and in rare cases a 1:1 ratio of carbohydrates to lean protein is needed for a short time (seven to twenty-one days) to get someone losing body fat. But remember, the calculations and advice are only as effective as the person's ability to follow it.

**Summary:**

Most people need a moderate amount of carbohydrates balanced with lean protein and good fats at most meals and snacks.

# CHAPTER THREE: Activity Level and Body Fat

Activity means exercise, and exercise means moving your body! My intention is to help you feel excited and motivated to be active, hopefully for the rest of your life! It is also a vital part of the *Eight Ways to Lose Your Blubber.*

You must treat exercise like brushing your teeth, shaving, flushing the toilet, or showering. Most of us do not get excited about these habits, but we do them anyway! Exercise must be an ongoing appointment on your calendar and part of your daily or weekly routine. I like the new slogan at my youngest son's elementary school—"No Excuses"—displayed on a billboard about not going to college in the future. I want you to use this slogan when you think about exercise.

Everyone should be active—every day. I hope to inspire you by giving you some important reasons and/or benefits for getting regular exercise.

- Two out of three adult Americans are overweight or obese.
- The risk of cancer, diabetes, heart disease, and death increases as your weight rises.

- Diabetes risk is eight times higher in overweight women and six times higher in overweight men.
- Obesity accelerates aging even more than smoking.
- Cognitive (mental) performance improves with exercise.
- Regular exercise in younger years reduces Alzheimer's risk by 60% later in life.
- Exercise helps with stress management.
- Daily activity reduces depression and anxiety symptoms. This is especially true in women.
- Neurotransmitters like serotonin are increased in the brain when you exercise.
- People who exercise have higher quality sleep.
- Muscle mass decreases 40%-50% between the ages of thirty and eighty.
- Physical activity increases muscle mass, therefore increasing the metabolic rate (your ability to burn calories).
- Active people report a better sex life and libido.
- Exercise, especially strength training, increases testosterone levels.
- Physical activity promotes self-esteem, and self-empowerment soars.
- Fit people reports higher incomes and job satisfaction.

## A Lifelong Habit

How can you make exercise a lifelong habit? If getting started on a regular exercise routine feels overwhelming, you might start by doing any kind of movement (walking, stretching, or using a yoga DVD) for ten to fifteen minutes every morning for at least three weeks. It generally takes three weeks to establish a new habit.

For those who have been inactive for a long period of time or may have a health concern, please consult with your physician before starting an exercise program. You may also consider hiring a certified personal trainer to help you develop a routine tailored to your needs and body fat loss or health goals.

Once you have established an exercise routine, make sure it includes all three of the main components of exercise: 1) cardiovascular/aerobic, 2) strength training/weight training, and 3) flexibility/stretching. Each component is important if you want good health, a strong body, good balance, a lower risk of injury, and lower body fat with a higher metabolic rate as you age.

Cardiovascular/aerobic exercise is important because it strengthens the heart, lungs, and circulatory system. It expends calories, reduces blood pressure, increases the good cholesterol levels in the body (HDL), and reduces clinical symptoms of anxiety, tension, and depression. Examples include walking fast, running, jumping rope, cycling, and swimming, taking an aerobics class, or following a dance DVD. What feels right for you? Choose the exercise you know you can do regularly.

Strength training and weight lifting aid in strengthening the bones and add muscle mass. One out of every four postmenopausal women is diagnosed with osteoporosis, a fairly preventable disease. As I stated earlier, after the age of twenty-five, we lose more than ½ pound of muscle every year of life. This is a choice but not inevitable! We want to keep every pound of muscle. It is the best natural antiaging strategy because muscle is metabolically active; fat is not! Strength training helps to assure body fat loss, not muscle loss during weight loss. Examples are circuit training with machines in a gym, free weight lifting with dumbbells and barbells, and exercises that use your whole body weight, such as push-ups. Start slow and be consistent. Remember, a new habit takes at least three weeks to establish for most of us anyway!

Flexibility and stretching help with body stability, allowing you to perform everyday chores and activities with ease, such as combing your hair, carrying the groceries, or climbing stairs. These exercises can help prevent injury and reduce stress around the joints that affects movement. Examples include yoga, Pilates, physical therapy exercises using a Bosu+ Ball, and calisthenics. Yoga is a great stretching exercise and can help to relax the body, bringing you back to a state of balance and peace. Ahh, breathe!

## Assessing Your Progress

Now that you understand why you should exercise, and what kind of exercise you can do, let's talk about how to assess your progress so you can physically and mentally see and feel how exercise has positively impacted your life beyond just losing or gaining pounds.

The following assessments will let you see your body's current state before you start or change any exercise routine and give you some parameters to monitor your progress. Sometimes it takes at least two to sixteen weeks (half a month to four months) before you can actually see body fat or weight changes, especially if you have any hormone imbalances. Record these assessments in your food diary or make a separate progress report and reevaluate every two to four weeks. Do as many of these assessments as possible to help you track your progress; the more successful you feel and the more changes you track, the more motivated you will be to continue.

- Record your weight. Weigh yourself on the same scale, at the same time, with the same clothes on or naked, **once a week.** Weighing yourself too often sabotages your progress.
- Check your Body Mass Index (BMI), which is weight in relation to your height (see BMI chart at the end of this chapter to obtain your BMI).
    - Healthy is 18.5-24.9. Risks start to increase when BMI goes above 23.
    - BMI is not a good assessment if you have a lot of muscle or are a football player or bodybuilder. Monitor your body fat in these cases! Muscle weighs more than fat.
- Measure the circumference of your waist (at the belly button—it doesn't move) and circumference of your hips (the largest part around your hips and butt). Use a tape measure.
    - Desired level for the waist for men is less than forty inches and for women should be less than thirty-five inches.
    - Take the inches of your waist and divide it by the inches of your hips. This number is called your waist to hip ratio. Men should be less than 1.0 and women should be less than 0.8.

- Inches lost. Are you losing inches? Use the tape measure to assess each of these body parts: one inner thigh (at the biggest point), chest, one bicep, waist, and hips.
- Assess body fat percent, pounds of fat, and pounds of muscle mass using a handheld device or scale method (both are bioelectric impedance analysis methods). Review chapter one.
  - o You can also assess your body fat through underwater weighing, DEXA (dual energy x-ray absorptiometry), or skin calipers. All assessment techniques have their advantages and disadvantages. The best advice I can give you is to use the same scale and system of remeasuring your body fat **every four weeks**, so you have a consistent system and can see progress.
- Assess hormones. Compare before and after exercise hormone levels of estradiol, progesterone, testosterone, cortisol, DHEA (through saliva testing), and serotonin (by urine testing) every two to six months, depending on your weight progress and symptoms.
- Take your blood pressure (daily or weekly), and your lipids (cholesterol) and glucose by a blood test every two to three months if you are losing weight and body fat and making serious food and exercise changes.

In addition to documenting the above tests and measurements in your food diary, you may want to record your weekly, monthly, and long-terms goals as well as your exercise sessions. While exercising, you can also monitor your heart rate and your calorie expenditure with a heart rate monitor watch, or wear a heart monitor belt. If you are using a pedometer, aim for at least 10,000 steps per day (about four miles). Lastly, assess how you are sleeping, your self-esteem, body confidence, and ability to manage stress. Record this information in your food diary and remember to celebrate successes!! We often pick on what we haven't done instead of being excited over what we have accomplished. Celebrate with a nonfood reward…new dress, round of golf, movie, mini vacation, massage, hiring a personal trainer, etc. ***Celebrate!***

**Meal and Snack Timing**

You have developed an exercise routine and are assessing your progress.

Now, I would like to talk about how meal timing and snack timing affect body fat loss, your weight, and exercise performance goals.

If you are hungry before you start to exercise, eat a small snack to avoid low energy and low blood sugar levels. You do not want to eat a big meal right before exercise unless you are hungry because the body will use the glucose it just broke down from the food you ate instead of breaking down body fat. So, if you are exercising less than sixty minutes, you can exercise on an empty stomach if it is early in the morning. If you feel nauseous, lightheaded, or get the sweats, try eating ½ banana, or a shake or something small like a Clementine orange that doesn't cause burping or stomach distress to your body.

After exercising sixty minutes or longer, you need to refuel your glycogen stores (storage form of carbohydrates in your muscles) and repair the little tears and stress you just caused to your muscles as soon as possible and preferably within thirty minutes. The best food recommendation I give is to eat a combination of carbohydrates and protein; this even applies for athletes and for a variety of sporting events. Some examples are a sandwich (2 pieces of whole-wheat or whole grain bread, 3 ounces chicken breast or 2-3 ounces tuna), 8-12 ounces of organic milk, a whey or Complete Protein Shake, made by NSA with a piece of fruit, low-fat or fat-free cottage cheese, and ½ cup of pineapple, or even a string cheese and 4-8 whole grain or gluten-free crackers.

## Body Fat

Focus on body fat loss and achieving a healthier body fat percentage range, not weight loss. Many times people lose muscle and water and little or no body fat. A higher body fat percentage increases all health risks and diseases. You will burn more calories when you have less body fat. You will also be firmer and your skin will be smoother with less cellulite. The more muscle and less body fat you have, the smaller size clothes you will wear even if you weigh more because muscle weighs more that fat. A person with an obese body fat percentage can typically lose ½% to 3% body fat per month, while others may only lose ½% to 2% body fat per month. Do not compare yourself to others; focus on your own progress.

If your primary goal is to gain weight, I want you to gain lean muscle mass, not extra body fat. There are many thin people who have higher body fat levels than overweight people that exercise on a regular basis. Think body fat loss, not weight loss. Also, many studies show that if you exercise regularly and are overweight, you are probably healthier than a thin person who doesn't exercise. So do not let not having a perfect weight stop you from exercising!

The following chart shows body fat target ranges. If you are out of range, work on general body fat reduction first, but set short, medium, and long-term goals to at least reach the acceptable category.

# Body Mass Index (BMI) Chart

| | Normal | | | | | | Overweight | | | | | Obese | | | | | | | | | | Extreme Obesity | | | | | | | | | | | | | | |
|---|---|---|---|---|---|---|---|---|---|---|---|---|---|---|---|---|---|---|---|---|---|---|---|---|---|---|---|---|---|---|---|---|---|---|---|---|
| BMI ($kg/m^2$) | 19 | 20 | 21 | 22 | 23 | 24 | 25 | 26 | 27 | 28 | 29 | 30 | 31 | 32 | 33 | 34 | 35 | 36 | 37 | 38 | 39 | 40 | 41 | 42 | 43 | 44 | 45 | 46 | 47 | 48 | 49 | 50 | 51 | 52 | 53 | 54 |
| Height (inches) | Body Weight (pounds) | | | | | | | | | | | | | | | | | | | | | | | | | | | | | | | | | | | |
| 4'10" (58") | 91 | 96 | 100 | 105 | 110 | 115 | 119 | 124 | 129 | 134 | 138 | 143 | 148 | 153 | 158 | 162 | 167 | 172 | 177 | 181 | 186 | 191 | 196 | 201 | 205 | 210 | 215 | 220 | 224 | 229 | 234 | 239 | 244 | 248 | 253 | 258 |
| 59 | 94 | 99 | 104 | 109 | 114 | 119 | 124 | 128 | 133 | 138 | 143 | 148 | 153 | 158 | 163 | 168 | 173 | 178 | 183 | 188 | 193 | 198 | 203 | 208 | 212 | 217 | 222 | 227 | 232 | 237 | 242 | 247 | 252 | 257 | 262 | 267 |
| 60 | 97 | 102 | 107 | 112 | 118 | 123 | 128 | 133 | 138 | 143 | 148 | 153 | 158 | 163 | 168 | 174 | 179 | 184 | 189 | 194 | 199 | 204 | 209 | 215 | 220 | 225 | 230 | 235 | 240 | 245 | 250 | 255 | 261 | 266 | 271 | 276 |
| 61 | 100 | 106 | 111 | 116 | 122 | 127 | 132 | 137 | 143 | 148 | 153 | 158 | 164 | 169 | 174 | 180 | 185 | 190 | 195 | 201 | 206 | 211 | 217 | 222 | 227 | 232 | 238 | 243 | 248 | 254 | 259 | 264 | 269 | 275 | 280 | 285 |
| 62 | 104 | 109 | 115 | 120 | 126 | 131 | 136 | 142 | 147 | 153 | 158 | 164 | 169 | 175 | 180 | 186 | 191 | 196 | 202 | 207 | 213 | 218 | 224 | 229 | 235 | 240 | 246 | 251 | 256 | 262 | 267 | 273 | 278 | 284 | 289 | 295 |
| 63 | 107 | 113 | 118 | 124 | 130 | 135 | 141 | 146 | 152 | 158 | 163 | 169 | 175 | 180 | 186 | 191 | 197 | 203 | 208 | 214 | 220 | 225 | 231 | 237 | 242 | 248 | 254 | 259 | 265 | 270 | 278 | 282 | 287 | 293 | 299 | 304 |
| 64 | 110 | 116 | 122 | 128 | 134 | 140 | 145 | 151 | 157 | 163 | 169 | 174 | 180 | 186 | 192 | 197 | 204 | 209 | 215 | 221 | 227 | 232 | 238 | 244 | 250 | 256 | 262 | 267 | 273 | 279 | 285 | 291 | 296 | 302 | 308 | 314 |
| 65 | 114 | 120 | 126 | 132 | 138 | 144 | 150 | 156 | 162 | 168 | 174 | 180 | 186 | 192 | 198 | 204 | 210 | 216 | 222 | 228 | 234 | 240 | 246 | 252 | 258 | 264 | 270 | 276 | 282 | 288 | 294 | 300 | 306 | 312 | 318 | 324 |
| 66 | 118 | 124 | 130 | 136 | 142 | 148 | 155 | 161 | 167 | 173 | 179 | 186 | 192 | 198 | 204 | 210 | 216 | 223 | 229 | 235 | 241 | 247 | 253 | 260 | 266 | 272 | 278 | 284 | 291 | 297 | 303 | 309 | 315 | 322 | 328 | 334 |
| 67 | 121 | 127 | 134 | 140 | 146 | 153 | 159 | 166 | 172 | 178 | 185 | 191 | 198 | 204 | 211 | 217 | 223 | 230 | 236 | 242 | 249 | 255 | 261 | 268 | 274 | 280 | 287 | 293 | 299 | 306 | 312 | 319 | 325 | 331 | 338 | 344 |
| 68 | 125 | 131 | 138 | 144 | 151 | 158 | 164 | 171 | 177 | 184 | 190 | 197 | 203 | 210 | 216 | 223 | 230 | 236 | 243 | 249 | 256 | 262 | 269 | 276 | 282 | 289 | 295 | 302 | 308 | 315 | 322 | 328 | 335 | 341 | 348 | 354 |
| 69 | 128 | 135 | 142 | 149 | 155 | 162 | 169 | 176 | 182 | 189 | 196 | 203 | 209 | 216 | 223 | 230 | 236 | 243 | 250 | 257 | 263 | 270 | 277 | 284 | 291 | 297 | 304 | 311 | 318 | 324 | 331 | 338 | 345 | 351 | 358 | 365 |
| 70 | 132 | 139 | 146 | 153 | 160 | 167 | 174 | 181 | 188 | 195 | 202 | 209 | 216 | 222 | 229 | 236 | 243 | 250 | 257 | 264 | 271 | 278 | 285 | 292 | 299 | 306 | 313 | 320 | 327 | 334 | 341 | 348 | 355 | 362 | 369 | 376 |
| 71 | 136 | 143 | 150 | 157 | 165 | 172 | 179 | 186 | 193 | 200 | 208 | 215 | 222 | 229 | 236 | 243 | 250 | 257 | 265 | 272 | 279 | 286 | 293 | 301 | 308 | 315 | 322 | 329 | 338 | 343 | 351 | 358 | 365 | 372 | 379 | 386 |
| 72 | 140 | 147 | 154 | 162 | 169 | 177 | 184 | 191 | 199 | 206 | 213 | 221 | 228 | 235 | 242 | 250 | 258 | 265 | 272 | 279 | 287 | 294 | 302 | 309 | 316 | 324 | 331 | 338 | 346 | 353 | 361 | 368 | 375 | 383 | 390 | 397 |
| 73 | 144 | 151 | 159 | 166 | 174 | 182 | 189 | 197 | 204 | 212 | 219 | 227 | 235 | 242 | 250 | 257 | 265 | 272 | 280 | 288 | 295 | 302 | 310 | 318 | 325 | 333 | 340 | 348 | 355 | 363 | 371 | 378 | 386 | 393 | 401 | 408 |
| 74 | 148 | 155 | 163 | 171 | 179 | 186 | 194 | 202 | 210 | 218 | 225 | 233 | 241 | 249 | 256 | 264 | 272 | 280 | 287 | 295 | 303 | 311 | 319 | 326 | 334 | 342 | 350 | 358 | 365 | 373 | 381 | 389 | 396 | 404 | 412 | 420 |
| 75 | 152 | 160 | 168 | 176 | 184 | 192 | 200 | 208 | 216 | 224 | 232 | 240 | 248 | 256 | 264 | 272 | 279 | 287 | 295 | 303 | 311 | 319 | 327 | 335 | 343 | 351 | 359 | 367 | 375 | 383 | 391 | 399 | 407 | 415 | 423 | 431 |
| 76 | 156 | 164 | 172 | 180 | 189 | 197 | 205 | 213 | 221 | 230 | 238 | 246 | 254 | 263 | 271 | 279 | 287 | 295 | 304 | 312 | 320 | 328 | 336 | 344 | 353 | 361 | 369 | 377 | 385 | 394 | 402 | 410 | 418 | 426 | 435 | 443 |

Source: *The Practical Guide to the Identification, Evaluation, and Treatment of Overweight and Obesity in Adults*. National Heart, Lung, and Blood Institute and North American Association for the Study of Obesity. Bethesda, MD: National Institutes of Health; 2000. NIH Publication number 00-4084, October 2000.

| Body Fat Percentage Categories | | |
|---|---|---|
| Classification | Women (% fat) | Men (% fat) |
| Essential Fat | 10-12% | 2-4% |
| Athletes | 14-20% | 6-13% |
| Fitness | 21-24% | 14-17% |
| Acceptable | 25-31% | 18-25% |
| Obese | 32%+ | 25%+ |

| Interpreting Body Mass Index | |
|---|---|
| **Weight Status** | **BMI** |
| Underweight | Below 18.5 |
| Normal | 18.5-24.9 |
| Overweight | 25.0-29.9 |
| Obese | 30.0 and above |

## Summary:

Exercise—*just do it!* Make exercise and daily activity a commitment, and be sure to focus on losing body fat, not weight loss.

# CHAPTER FOUR: Thyroid Hormones, Insulin, and Glucose

## Thyroid Hormones

This chapter will teach you how to balance your thyroid, insulin, and glucose imbalance. I have found that 50% of my clients have undiagnosed or improperly treated thyroid, insulin, or glucose issues that can affect their body fat goals. Any imbalance in thyroid markers (blood tests) can cause increased body fat and negative symptoms.

Let's begin with the thyroid gland. The thyroid gland is a two-lobed gland that wraps around the trachea and is located at the base of the neck. It secretes two important hormones: thyroxine, which regulates how you burn calories, and calcitonin, which forms bones. It is fairly easy to diagnose and balance your thyroid with the right blood tests and other individualized recommendations.

Request the following blood tests to assess your thyroid properly if you have symptoms of fatigue or depression or can't lose body fat. If you do not have any of these symptoms, a TSH screening is probably adequate.

1) **TSH** (thyroid stimulating hormone). TSH is a hormone secreted by the pituitary gland that stimulates the thyroid gland. Hyperthyroidism is the diagnosis given when the TSH level is decreased and usually results in weight loss. Hypothyroidism is the diagnosis when the TSH level is elevated usually resulting in weight gain, however, you can be diagnosed with hyperthyroidism and exhibit hypothyroidism symptoms.
2) **T4, Free** (thyroxine). In 95% of the cases, when Free T4 is increased, the condition is hyperthyroidism, and if T4 is low, then the condition is hypothyroidism.
3) **T3, Total** (triiodothyonine). This determines whether the thyroid is functioning properly. T3 tests can be helpful to monitor a known thyroid condition and to help monitor the effectiveness of treatment for hyperthyroidism.
4) **T3, Free** (triiodothyronine). This shows only the active T3 in your body. It is not influenced by binding hormones, which we will discuss in upcoming chapters. It helps determine what kind of prescription medication may be best. In my experience, patients with low T3, free, levels often have higher LDL (low-density lipoprotein) levels, fatigue, depression, and weight gain.
5) **TPO** (thyroid peroxidase antibodies). An enzyme found in the thyroid gland, it plays an important role in the production of thyroid hormones. If you have elevated levels, it may indicate an autoimmune disorder such as Hashimoto's disease or Graves' disease, or even a future thyroid disorder.
6) **Thyroglobulin Panel** (includes thyroglobulin antibodies and thyroglobulin). Thyroglobulin is a thyroid protein that is the precursor to iodine-containing hormones. Again, elevated levels can indicate a future thyroid

disorder. In my practice, patients with higher than normal levels of TPO and thyroglobulin antibodies and thyroglobulin levels can reduce them with adequate vitamin D3 (cholecalciferol) and with iodine/potassium iodide supplements, which are both available over-the-counter.

7) **Spot and 24 Hour Iodine Test:** This is a urine test that helps to determine an iodine deficiency. Iodine aids in the production of thyroid hormones, such as thyroxine. Iodine helps to maintain a normal metabolism.

** Testing for Reverse T3 may also be done, but my experience and that of many thyroid experts that I work with have not found this test to be helpful.

These tests help you determine if the thyroid is functioning at high or low levels, or if you have a possible autoimmune issue or future thyroid disorder, all of which can affect moods, energy, weight gain or weight loss, and body fat. When you get these test results, it helps your doctor prescribe the right medication. Unfortunately, most patients are put on Synthyroid (levothyroxine sodium tablets) based on assessing TSH and Free T4 levels, and this does not always give the complete picture. If you have been on any thyroid medication or are newly diagnosed with a thyroid condition, make sure you have all the above blood tests done, plus a thyroid ultrasound and bone density test, within one year of diagnosis. This holds true even if you have been on medication for a long time and still are experiencing body fat challenges or symptoms of fatigue, depression, and feel cold all the time.

There are many factors that can cause a thyroid condition, one being stress. For example, in 2004 I was diagnosed with hyperthyroidism (underactive) with hypothyroidism (over-active) symptoms. I was experiencing fatigue all day, even during and after exercise, an inner feeling of despair, horrible muscle pain with exercise, extreme coldness, sleep disturbances, fast weight gain, and increased body fat. My endocrinologist and I agreed that my thyroid dysfunction probably resulted from high levels of stress. My stressors at the time started after a tubal ligation (any surgery stresses the body), a recent divorce, working more than sixty hours a week, caring for my two active boys, and training for a marathon. I have counseled hundreds of men and women who have experienced similar situations. By 2006 I was off thyroid medication by balancing all my hormones, supplementing with iodine and potassium to match my testing results, which showed low levels, and by reducing my work and high exercise schedule.

**Summary:**

The thyroid can affect your energy levels, weight, body fat, or moods. See your physician or endocrinologist (doctor who specializes in hormones) to get the right blood tests, assessments, and medication that fits your blood work. Keep in mind that it takes thyroid medication at least seven to ten days and sometimes up to four weeks to provide maximum results.

**Additional Resources:**

*The Thyroid Solution,* Ridha Arem, M.D.
*Hypothyroidism, Type 2,* Mark Starr, M.D.
*Overcoming Thyroid Disorder,* David Brownstein, M.D.

## Insulin and Glucose Issues

Elevated insulin and glucose (sugar) play a role in body fat and weight because they affect how the body breaks down carbohydrates. If you can't break down carbohydrates properly, your body fat goes up. The causes of elevated glucose and insulin include one or all of the following: inactivity, high cortisol levels, low DHEA levels, infections, obesity, a big waist circumference, poor nutrition, high progesterone, high testosterone in women and low testosterone in men, disturbed sleep, hypothyroidism, and/or excessive alcohol consumption. Symptoms of high insulin and glucose can include weight gain, abdominal obesity, fatigue, crabbiness, sugar cravings, neuropathy (needle like pain in toes, feet, and legs), inconsistent blood pressure, water retention, inflammation, and depression.

**To identify high insulin, measure these markers with a blood test:**

1) Fasting insulin. Ideal levels are less than 10. (If your doctor will not agree to a fasting insulin test, then do numbers two or three.)
2) Fasting lipid profile. Take your triglyceride value divided by your HDL (high density lipoprotein) value. A good triglyceride: HDL ratio is between 2 and 4. (This is a general guideline. It is always better to be too low than too high when assessing insulin.)

**For example, if your triglyceride level is 110 and your HDL is 59, you would divide 110 by 59 to get 2; this is an acceptable level, indicating that you probably do not have high insulin levels.

3) Fasting lipid profile. Look at your level of triglycerides and make sure they stay below 130. A level over 130 could be a red flag for rising insulin levels.

**To identify elevated glucose, measure these markers with a blood test:**

1) Fasting glucose. Ideal levels are between 70 and 99.
2) Hemoglobin A1C percent. This is not a fasting test. If you are diabetic, a reading of 6% or less is great. If you are not diabetic, this level should be in the 5% ranges.
    a. 6% = approximately 124 glucose level
    b. 5% = approximately 92.4 glucose level
    c. 4% = approximately 60.7 glucose level
3) Oral Glucose Tolerance Test (OGTT): a glucose solution is given and glucose is tested by serum testing in intervals. This test measures the body's ability to use sugar.

In 2007, I counseled ten people between the ages of nine and fifty-five who were overlooked for insulin resistance. All of these patients had a normal fasting glucose level, but fasting insulin levels were above 10. They all had abdominal obesity, elevated cortisol levels, could not lose body fat, and felt sluggish after eating any carbohydrate-containing foods. I also had another dozen patients that all had the same symptoms of impaired glucose plus neuropathy (pins and needles in the feet). They were all diabetic and did not know it. Their fasting glucose test showed levels of glucose above 126, and all had a hemoglobin A1C above 6%. Many others had some levels of prediabetes. This means they had a fasting glucose between 100 and 126. Their doctors did not tell them they were prediabetic or suggest seeing a dietitian or losing weight. Almost all cases of prediabetes become diabetes in the future. Take control of your outcome, make sure you ask for a copy of your blood tests, and ask questions! No one will take care of your body as well as you. I hope these examples and reference ranges help you demand the right assessments and tests to then determine what lifestyle and other treatment and balancing you need to take control of now!

Here are the steps to keep normal insulin and glucose levels.

1) Eat four to six minimeals per day.
2) Eat every two to three hours, but never go longer than four hours in between meals.
3) Limit carbohydrates to two to three servings per meal and one to two servings per snack. (Refer back to chapter one.)
4) Eat a protein source at each meal, such as meat, poultry, lentils, beans, cheese, eggs, seafood, protein bars, or whey, soy, hemp, or egg white protein shakes. (Again, refer back to chapter one.)
5) Avoid or limit sugar, candy, honey, jelly, syrup, regular soda, doughnuts, pastries, sweet muffins, sweetened cereals, pies, cakes, puddings, and alcohol.

**If these foods are desired, eat a small serving, use sugar-free syrups, or eat a lean protein source with these foods.

6) Eat a good breakfast every day, such as:
    - 20 to 30 grams whey, soy, or egg white protein shake made with ½ cup of fruit and 8 ounces of water or skim milk;
    - high-fiber cereal (6 to 14 grams of fiber) made with a whey, soy or egg white shake in place of milk;
    - 2 eggs and 1 slice of toast spread thin with peanut butter;

- Omelet made with ½ cup of Egg Beaters or egg whites only, ¼ cup of low-fat shredded cheese, and some sautéed vegetables or salsa.

7) Keep your lunch and dinner choices healthy, such as:
   - ½ cup of tuna salad made with fat-free mayo, fat-free cottage cheese, or plain yogurt on whole wheat bread;
   - 3 ounces of grilled chicken and ¼ cup to ½ cup of kidney beans over a bed of spinach, romaine lettuce, or Boston green leaf lettuce;
   - 3 ounces of sirloin steak with 1 cup of green beans and ½ cup rice;
   - 3 ounces of turkey wrapped in a big romaine lettuce leaf.

8) Snack ideas:
   - 2 tablespoons-4 tablespoons of peanuts or other nuts or seeds;
   - 1/3 cup of soy nuts;
   - ¼ cup of edamame;
   - ½ cup of fat-free cottage cheese with ½ cup of fresh fruit;
   - Protein bar with adequate protein and carbohydrates. Ideally the bar should contain a carbohydrate-to-protein ratio between 2:1 or 1:1 (example: 20 grams carbohydrates and 10 grams protein, so this is a 2:1 ratio);
   - 1 ounce of cheese and 4 to 8 whole grain crackers;
   - Dried beef jerky or ostrich meat and ½ a muffin.

Additional tips/treatments for elevated insulin or glucose levels:

1) Lower intake of total carbohydrates.
   - Try lower glycemic index foods such as berries, beans, and bran cereals. Lower glycemic foods may not raise the blood sugar as much or as fast as high glycemic foods, such as white bread, potatoes, candy, and most junk foods.
   - Eat high-fiber carbohydrates such as lentils, beans, and vegetables.
   - Eat lean protein with each meal and each snack.
   - Keep your total carbohydrate percent to less than 50% (see chapter two).
2) Lose weight, and lower your body fat to 25% or less (see chapter two).
3) Exercise, exercise, exercise. The more muscle and the less body fat you have, the easier your body can use insulin and glucose.
4) Try herbs and other supplements such as:
   - Juice Plus and Vineyard Blend capsules by NSA;
   - Insinase, by Metagenics;
   - Cinnamon, Gymnema Sylvester, fenugreek, chromium, D3, eicosapentaenoic acid (EPA) containing fish oil, and several other supplements.

     (See your qualified, licensed health professional or registered dietitian for the highest quality brands, dosages, and interaction information when using herbs or dietary supplements. Juice Plus is a whole food concentrate, therefore it is safe.)
5) Many prescription medications are available for elevated glucose. See your doctor for choices. The most popular prescription medication for elevated insulin is called Metformin. If you decide to take Metformin, be sure to

assess your B12 levels yearly, since this drug can cause a B12 deficiency.

Changing your elevated insulin and glucose levels and losing body fat may take at least three to twelve months. Be patient!

**Summary:**

High insulin and glucose levels contribute to body fat and weight. If you suspect elevated levels, assess your fasting glucose, insulin and hemoglobin A1C by a blood test, start monitoring your carbohydrate intake, get plenty of exercise, and lose body fat.

# CHAPTER FIVE: Estrogen, Progesterone, and Testosterone; Hormone Conditions and Testing

Hormones affect everything. The purpose of this chapter is to help you weed through difficult hormone terminology, define hormones, learn how to best assess them, and then find the correct treatment for your body. Hormones are vital to aging elegantly, feeling energetic, and maintaining a healthy body fat level. Hormones affect everything. I am especially excited about this chapter because knowing this information has changed many of my patients' lives as well as my perspective on health and illness.

Hormones affect our body fat and overall well-being. Hormones are made of molecules called proteins or peptides. Hormones are made in one cell and send messages to other cells. We will discuss hormone conditions, how to test your hormone levels, how they affect your body fat and weight, and what to do about any imbalances you find through testing.

Let's start by going over some hormone conditions, syndromes, and deficiencies and how they affect body fat and weight:

**Premenstrual syndrome**, often referred to as PMS, is a syndrome that occurs prior to the beginning of menstruation and ends a few days after menstruation starts. It can contribute to carbohydrate binge eating, especially sweets, and to water weight, bloating, and fatigue.

**Perimenopause** is a break in the menstrual cycle that usually starts between ages 35 and 55. It can cause weight gain around the stomach. If sleep disturbances occur, this can contribute to the hormone imbalances in ghrenlin and leptin which increase appetite. Poor sleep also increases the adrenal hormone called cortisol that causes waist fat and elevated insulin.

**Postmenopause** is the term used for the permanent end of the menstrual cycle for at least twelve consecutive months. The same symptoms apply as with perimenopause but can be more drastic.

**Andropause** is a drop in a man's hormone levels. This occurs more gradually in men than menopause in women and usually starts between the ages of 40 and 55. The waist expands and the body shape takes the form of an apple. Testosterone and DHEA (dehydroepiandrosterone) levels often drop and contribute to muscle loss.

**Estrogen dominance** refers to estradiol levels that are high due to a decline in progesterone levels. This often occurs with PMS, perimenopause, insulin resistance, and prolonged stress of any kind, especially after pregnancy. Symptoms may include weight gain and an increase in body fat, bloating, irregular periods, breast tenderness, mood swings, food cravings, and a lowered sex drive. Estrogen dominance is often associated with cysts and fibroids.

**Adrenal Fatigue Syndrome** occurs when the adrenal glands are under enormous stress. This can be any kind of stress: poor nutrition, biochemical, emotional, low hormones, or environmental. The adrenals become over stimulated, and then DHEA and cortisol rise and eventually bottom out, causing weight gain, a slower metabolism, fatigue, depression, anxiety, and aches and pain that often prevent you from exercising. Even thinking can be affected, causing you to have less willpower, motivation, and drive to choose healthy foods and get regular activity. See the next chapter for more information.

**25-hydroxy vitamin D3** deficient levels can contribute to bone weakening, depression, fatigue, autoimmune issues such as lupus and multiple sclerosis (MS), gastrointestinal conditions such as Crohn's disease, high blood pressure, and heart disease. Vitamin D3 works like a hormone, not a vitamin. Research regarding 25-hydroxy D3 has uncovered the most exciting and helpful nutrition information that I have learned in the last five years. The research keeps showing more and more functions of this vitamin that acts like a hormone! Chapter seven makes specific recommendations for testing and supplementing.

Next we will describe the three main hormones that affect our body fat, weight, and moods our entire life. This chapter will explain some, but not all, of the symptoms associated with imbalances of these hormones.

Let's first define these major hormones:

### Estrogen

There are three types of estrogen: estrone (E1), estradiol (E2), and estriol E3. They are produced in the ovaries, fat cells, the liver, and the adrenal glands. The symptoms most commonly reported by women are often related to estradiol, such as hot flashes, insomnia, depression, abdominal weight gain, increased body fat, and urinary changes.

### Progesterone

This hormone is produced in many places in the body, and its functions include maintaining a pregnancy, having a healthy sexual desire, and preventing disorders that lead to fatigue, endometrial growth, breast cancer, depression, sleep disturbances, and estrogen dominance that causes increased body fat.

### Testosterone

Testosterone is a steroid hormone. The ovaries produce half of the testosterone in women, and the testes secrete testosterone in men. This hormone influences insulin levels, sexual desire, maintaining a healthy bone density and body fat.

## A Closer Look at Hormones

We are defining these hormones because they contribute to body fat and well-being. As mentioned earlier, the body produces three types of estrogen.The first is **Estrone (E1)**. It is made in our body fat and ovaries. Its production often increases with perimenopause, which can increase your risk of breast cancer. Even if you have low levels of E1, I do not recommend using estrone in any bioidentical hormone therapy treatments. I would not recommend using Tri-est (a combination of three estrogens: estradiol, estriol, and estrone). Estrone is generally not used by anyone having a personal or family risk of breast cancer.

**Estradiol (E2)** has over four hundred functions in the body, so I won't be listing all of them. If you want to explore more, read some of the references I provide at the end of this chapter. A thickening of the waist and irregular sleep patterns are two problems that can be avoided by maintaining adequate E2 levels.

Let's look at the tornado of events that occur when just inadequate estradiol levels are present: first, you have hot flashes, they wake you up, cortisol rises, this wakes you up again, then you get less than five hours of straight sleep, and grehlin and leptin, two other hormones in the stomach, are disturbed. They stimulate appetite, causing you to eat more carbohydrates. Insulin rises, cortisol follows, creating inflammation and more carbohydrate cravings, causing you to have a bigger waist and body fat with less willpower to avoid binging on carbohydrates. Now you wake up tired and crabby, and you are too tired to exercise, which again contributes to more weight gain. Now imagine what happens when this goes on for months or, in many of my patients' cases, for years...a disaster.

**Estriol (E3)**Treatment for low estradiol is usually successful with a second estrogen called estriol (E3).A formula such as this, compounded by a pharmacy, is usually called Bi-est (two estrogens).

Estriol (E3) is a somewhat weak hormone. It is produced in high amounts during pregnancy. It typically doesn't build up the endometrial wall, and can help with peri- and post-menopausal symptoms such as vaginal dryness and urinary incontinence. It doesn't have much to do with body fat directly; however, estradiol works better in conjunction with estriol. For example, most patients with estradiol deficiency have an estriol deficiency, too, and balance between these two estrogens reduces stress in the body, therefore helping to lose body fat. Stress of any kind usually increases body fat.

You will find different and often very strong opinions about which form of hormones to take in the many books written about hormone imbalances. My belief, proven by experience, is that each patient should be treated as unique with an individualized treatment plan to meet her specific needs. The patient should be offered options of oral, topical, patch, sublingual, bioidentical and synthetic treatments, and be made aware of the negatives and positives about each hormone.

Let's not forget about men. Men also produce estradiol. When estradiol is elevated in a man, it can contribute to prostate issues and waist fat and, often, increased levels of an enzyme called aromatase. For this reason it is very important to omit or limit all alcohol, lose body fat, and check for medications that can elevate levels of estradiol. Common medications that increase estradiol in men include antifungal treatments, cholesterol-lowering medications, blood pressure drugs, antibiotics, heartburn medications, and over-the-counter pain relievers such as aspirin and ibuprofen.

Ask your health care provider to evaluate your current medication list. Lifestyle changes and treatment can include losing body fat; taking short term high doses of vitamin C; eating more cruciferous vegetables (kale, broccoli, etc.), raw food salads, and green smoothies; drinking vegetable juices; adding whole food supplementation like Juice Plus by NSA; herbal supplements; and pharmacy compounded progesterone, chrysin, and Arimidex.

If estrogen treatment of any kind is not desirable for health reasons such as a high cancer risk, then soy, black cohosh, flax seed (lignans), dong quai, and bioflavonoids found in some herbs and fruits, and whole food supplementation are recommended, especially for menopausal symptoms. All natural treatments have pros and cons and potential medication and disease interactions, so consult a health-care practitioner who has herbal and vitamin knowledge. This could be an integrative dietitian, clinical nutritionist, a person trained in functional medicine, or a compounding pharmacist.

## Progesterone

Next we are going to talk about progesterone, because it affects body fat and moods. Progesterone deficiency can contribute to PMS and cause problems at any age, particularly after a pregnancy or tubal ligation, or during peri- or postmenopause. When progesterone levels drop or when estradiol levels are high relative to progesterone, estrogen dominance can occur, and this affects body fat and waist circumference.

**Polycystic ovary syndrome (PCOS)** is an endocrine disorder that can lead to infertility, with symptoms including missed or irregular periods and cysts on the ovaries. Women with PCOS often have estrogen dominance and insulin resistance. When progesterone stays low, abdominal fat, fatigue, depression, sleep disturbances, and a lowered libido set in. PCOS patients come in very frustrated with their weight gain, hair growth, and diabetes. The traditional treatment of this disorder may include birth control, synthetic hormone therapy, and other prescription medications, such as Metformin. There are other options such as nutrition, exercise, body fat loss, and assessing estradiol, progesterone, and testosterone which can alleviate PCOS and many or all of its symptoms and progression.

The integrative prescription treatment as a part of PCOS I recommend with the patient's gynecologist include bio-identical progesterone made into an oral treatment (pills or capsules), or lotions and creams applied to the skin or labia, fit to that patient's hormonal levels. Initial testing of progesterone levels, and retesting of serum or saliva progesterone levels in four to sixteen weeks, is imperative.

**PMS and low or high estradiol**. The conditions can cause binge eating, cravings, and mood disturbances that can go on for many, many years. The typical medical treatments include birth control, antidepressants, and sleep aids. But listen up—these do not have to be the first treatment option!

**Symptoms of PMS include, but are not limited to:**

Irregular, unpredictable, or heavy menstrual cycles
Feeling tense and irritable
Being anxious and overly worried
Mood changes, including heightened sensitivity and crying easily
Depression
Headaches
Water retention
Weight gain
Bloating
Breast tenderness
Binge eating

These treatments are the integrative therapies that I recommend to try for PMS or estradiol imbalances. These make more sense because they do no harm—which is my wish for everyone!

1) **Practice clean nutrition**: restrict salt, caffeinated beverages, fried and fatty foods, and all forms of refined sugars.
2) **Try natural supplements** first before using prescription medications:
    - Use a whole food supplement with supportive medical evidence, such as Juice Plus capsules, because most multiple vitamin/minerals do not contain the right form and dosage for your needs or safety.
    - Get at least 1,000 to 1,200 milligrams per day of calcium from food and calcium citrate or hydroxyapatite. These forms are digested better, won't interact

with most medications, can be taken on an empty stomach, and won't cause constipation.According to the American Journal of Obstetrics and Gynecology (179: 444, 1998), 1,200 mg of calcium reduced PMS symptoms by 52%. I rarely see any young or older women getting adequate calcium per day, so this is an area many women need to evaluate.

Take enough Omega 3 and Omega 6 fatty acids. Between 1 and 4 grams of fish oil containing EPA and DHA can help with hormonal balance. Fish oil reduces inflammation, which contributes to a higher body fat and can lower high triglycerides, which lowers the risk if high insulin levels and elevated glucose.

- About 2 to 4 grams of evening primrose oil per day can also help to relieve breast tenderness and PMS symptoms, especially when taken with 1,000-1,200 mg of calcium/day.
- Taking between 500 and 1,000 mg, three times a day, of the herb called vitex/chasteberry can increase progesterone and decrease estradiol, while easing breast pain and other symptoms of PMS. However, vitex may interfere with oral contraceptives and hormone replacement. If other hormonal imbalances are suspected, do not take vitex until you know your levels of estradiol, progesterone, and testosterone based on saliva testing. Until you have this information, you could fix one symptom and add three more by taking vitex. It has been my experience that vitex is put into many women's hormonal dietary supplement formulas and

sometimes actually lowers a hormone that is already low.

- Individual vitamins and minerals can be helpful. For example, 400 to 1,000 mg of magnesium and 25,000 IU of vitamin A can help with excessive menstrual bleeding. Folic acid, vitamin B6 (pyridoxine) at 25 to 100 mg a day), and B12 can also be helpful. But all of these have guidelines and cautions for use. Your best source of guidance on these is to consult with an integrative health practitioner, not someone who reads health magazines or the eighteen-year-old that waits on you at a local health food or vitamin store, because these supplements can cause diarrhea, liver toxicity, and other symptoms.

3) Other helpful tools are available. Louise Hay, one of my favorite authors, has a great reference book called *Heal Your Body*. She states that the probable emotional causes of PMS is "allowing confusion to rein. Giving power to outside influences. Rejection of the feminine processes." Her suggested affirmation is to say: "I now take charge of my mind and my life. I am a powerful, dynamic woman! Every part of my body functions perfectly. I love me." Saying this affirmation daily and frequently when experiencing PMS can be very helpful. I recommend many integrative healing techniques that will be explored further in chapter eight.

### Testosterone

Testosterone is an androgen, or male hormone, but, yes, women have it, too. Testosterone production decreases at approximately 1% a year after the age of forty for males.

However, men undergo a more gradual hormonal change with aging than women and are fertile most of their life. So, watch out, perimenopausal ladies!

Saliva and blood hormone testing can assess testosterone levels so that bioidentical choices or testosterone patches, gels, lotions, and capsules can be prescribed. But be careful to check for the levels of a protein called sex hormone binding globulin (SHBG) and albumin if only using blood testing. A normal blood test may not indicate normal levels of "free" testosterone, which can affect daily moods, libido, erections, and lean muscle mass, therefore body fat.

Testosterone preserves that precious lean tissue called muscle that men have more of than women. Elevated levels of testosterone can cause irritability, moodiness, and insulin resistance. Low testosterone and low free testosterone increase C-reactive protein (CRP), Il-6, which can contribute to inflammation and disease, a loss of lean muscle mass and bone, feeling less motivated, and having less sexual drive and desire to exercise.

The good news is that exercise, especially weight-bearing exercise increases testosterone levels, as does taking DHEA only if you are a woman with deficient levels of DHEA and testosterone. Among my patients I have only one or two women per year that I recommend trying some topical testosterone. But men with erectile dysfunction and low levels of testosterone benefit greatly with a compounded transdermal or skin form of testosterone replacement. This preserves lean muscle.

A more natural approach to libido and arousal for men may include herbs such as ginkgo, Asian or Panax ginseng, yohimbe, maca, or the amino acid arginine. Any of these can increase blood flow to the penis and enhance sexual arousal. Yohimbe has been rated as "possibly effective" for erectile and sexual dysfunction by the Natural Medicine Comprehensive Database. DHEA and HGH (human growth hormone) dietary supplements and prescription hormones are other possible options, but I highly recommend guidance from a health professional combined with hormone testing and, if needed, high-quality supplements based on individual needs, because I have seen insulin resistance, diabetes, hair growth, acne, and severe irritability.

If taking supplements, watch for interactions with prescription medications. For example, do not take ginkgo with blood thinners; yohimbe can cause irritability, anxiety, and sleep disturbances; and Asian ginseng can elevate blood pressure and provoke insomnia. These recommendations may perplex you since this book is mainly concerned about weight loss. However, men's weight and health are greatly affected by their libido and testosterone levels.

**Summary:**

Estrogens, progesterone, and testosterone play a huge, daily role in weight maintenance, moods, health, and general well-being. The secret of hormone balancing at any age is obtaining the proper individualized hormone testing, nutritional support, traditional prescription therapy, and bioidentical hormone therapy if needed. Integrative options and stress reduction are also highly recommended.

**Assessing Hormones:**

Now that you know what hormones are and what integrative options to try or read more about, let's talk about hormone testing. To assess these hormone conditions, consult your health practitioner. Do not use a Web site or any over-the-counter hormone like progesterone or DHEA, no matter how good or popular the advertising says it is. I have witnessed weight gain of ten or more pounds, hypothyroidism, excessive bleeding, swollen ovaries, and worsened depression and fatigue in people who take these treatments on their own.

Ask your practitioner to test all your hormones, not just progesterone and estradiol, but all the ones listed in this book. If your practitioner uses only supplements, over-the-counter progesterone, or prescription drugs alone to solve your issues, keep looking for better help. To reduce depression and anxiety, some people need bioidentical estrogens, blood and saliva testing, exercise, nutrition or behavioral counseling, and usually a combination of all of these. Achieving balance, well-being, and good health, and avoiding a disease such as osteoporosis, should be high on anyone's wish list, especially yours.

I have found that the doctors and health practitioners who communicate well and work together for your best interests have patients with a much higher success rate. When I have a new patient, I always communicate with her gynecologist, general physician, or health practitioner—whoever is most important to her and her situation. I see a 90% to 95% success rate in symptoms and weight loss with my patients who allow me to communicate with their health practitioners versus a 50% or less success rate with those who don't.

So, how do you test for these conditions? First, a lot of subjective questioning should occur. You should do the talking first, and then the practitioner should ask you a lot of questions to learn about your physical, emotional, nutritional, sleep, lifestyle, exercise, and many private conditions such as your sex drive, erections, and vaginal dryness, along with your medical, prescription, surgery, menstrual cycle, and over-the-counter supplement history. Then saliva, blood, and possibly urine testing and hair analysis should be ordered. If your heath practitioner will not assess your hormone levels, then find one who will.

Unless you are experiencing severe symptoms, do not start on anything except nutritional support, and immediately begin implementing small lifestyle changes such as reducing or omitting all caffeine and alcohol. Wait for your test results to come back before taking any hormones of any kind. Most test results take a minimum of three days and up to four weeks to get back.

Of course, if your health is in serious jeopardy, follow your physician's recommendations. But be sure to ask about side effects, read information about your condition, and read the insert of any pharmaceutical drug you're asked to take. You are the one most responsible for your body, so be your own health advocate.

## Saliva, Urine and Blood Testing

Saliva hormone testing is the optimal way to measure hormone levels of estradiol, estriol, progesterone, testosterone,

DHEA, and cortisol. Saliva contains hormones in their free or unbound state. Do you feel the same every day? Of course not. Saliva testing has the following benefits: it is done in your home, it is noninvasive, and you can take samples at different times of the day or night, as well as different days of the menstrual cycle.

Testing hormones through a blood test is not always as accurate as saliva testing. Many people eat terribly, experience enormous stress, and take prescription medications. These factors can interfere with testing these hormones by blood. To decide where to order your saliva testing, ask your practitioner what his or her success rate is and if he or she has been using saliva testing for a year or more. After your test results are back, the recommendations should be individualized for you based on your health, nutrition status, hormone levels, and symptoms determined from the original, detailed, subjective questioning, not a computerized report.

Many practitioners are unwilling to recommend saliva testing because often insurance doesn't cover the testing. In my experience, it takes at least forty-five to seventy-five minutes to collect all the subjective information needed from the patient; doctors do not have this amount time to give during an appointment. Choosing the right saliva kit also requires extra time and least five to ten minutes of instructions.

It is unfortunate that saliva testing to assess hormones is not used regularly. I have so many cases of patients' blood tests showing normal hormone levels, only to have the woman or man suffer for years afterward. Yet, when we test their saliva, it shows deficiencies or imbalances that match their symptoms. So many patients sit and cry in my office because they finally feel relieved that they are not crazy and that they finally can get the right treatment. Once you start any treatment, you must get retested every two to six months until you achieve balance, then every year for minor adjustments and good health.

Patients in this situation are so disenchanted about why they didn't know about saliva testing sooner, why their doctor couldn't help them, and why the prescription medications were given in the first place. I encourage every man and woman to share this information and success with their health practitioners. Learn even more about it by reading and going to seminars. But above all, share this information with your friends and family.

We also need to keep in mind that blood (serum) testing is the preferred method for certain conditions, including thyroid imbalance, vitamin D3 deficiency, and insulin and glucose issues. I want to mention cholesterol here because it is a steroid hormone. Cholesterol testing should also be done by blood if hormone issues are suspected based on typical symptoms, or a hysterectomy, weight gain, or andropause. Sometimes blood and saliva testing for female and male hormone levels is helpful. Again, this is where individualization comes into play for all patients.

Hair tissue mineral analysis (HTMA) often gets some flack from the traditional medical community. Yet I have seen so many cases of unsolved fatigue, anxiety, depression, eating disorders, ADD, and ADHD improve after testing of minerals by hair confirmed the analysis. Athletes and people who exercise for ninety minutes or more, five days a week or more, also benefit from HTMA due to their mineral losses in sweat and extensive muscle and nerve conduction use. It is an additional option or an option for later if all symptoms aren't improved.

Urine testing can be helpful for neurotransmitter levels such as serotonin, dopamine, and epinephrine, and a few practitioners use urine testing for hormone testing. Serotonin is one of the main neurotransmitters in the brain that can affect sleep, moods, and appetite, including carbohydrate cravings. Neurotransmitters are discussed further in the next chapter.

**Summary:**

Test all your female and male hormones and get individualized treatment that fits your medical history, your levels, and symptoms, and follow a plan that you feel intuitively comfortable doing. Please remember to retest your hormone appropriately! Do not just go by symptoms!

**Additional Resources:**

*Renew Your Life through Hormone Balancing*, Valerie Early, 2007, audio CD, 847-985-1200, www.nutritionconnectionbalance.com

*Natural Hormone Replacement: For Women Over 45*, Dr. J. Wright and J. Morgenthaler.

*Natural Woman, Natural Menopause*, C. Conrad and M. Laux

*The Wisdom of Menopause*, Dr. C. Northrup
*What Your Doctor May Not Tell You about Breast Cancer*, Dr. J. Lee, V. Hopkins, and D. Zava
*Safe Estrogen*, Edward Conley
*Perfect Balance*, Robert Greene

# CHAPTER SIX: The Adrenals: Cortisol and DHEA and the Neurotransmitters

The adrenal glands help the body adapt to all kinds of stress. They are located over the kidneys and secrete many hormones, including aldosterone, cortisol, dopamine, DHEA, progesterone, estradiol, epinephrine, nor epinephrine, and dopamine.

I decided to devote a whole chapter to adrenals and neurotransmitters because of the drastic increase I've seen in the last six years in new patients with problems related to disturbed cortisol, DHEA, and serotonin levels.

I can't help but reinforce how deeply our lifestyles affect our health. Look at the average American routine: we don't value good nutrition, most people are underactive, we regularly stay up after midnight, we drink fancy coffees all day, and most of us multitask from morning to bedtime. We set ourselves up for stress, which can occur from poor eating, an illness like the flu or chronic infection, emotional upsets, environmental issues, hormonal imbalances, or any combination of these.

All of these lifestyle choices force our bodies to react. And that's why the incidences of adrenal fatigue are escalating. Symptoms of adrenal fatigue include exhaustion, trouble waking up in the morning, more fatigue after exercise, changes in nutrient metabolism and body shape, depression, anxiety, cognitive confusion and fogginess, decreased sex drive, sleep disturbances, and cravings for salt and sugar.

**Assessment:** The best way to determine if you have any adrenal disorder is through a thorough, multistep process that includes a subjective and objective assessment of your situation with a health practitioner familiar with adrenal fatigue. This should include asking many questions about your symptoms, medical history, current prescriptions and OTC supplements, daily schedule the last one to two years, and a typical food and exercise intake. After about forty-five minutes of questioning or more, an experienced health practitioner can put together an individualized saliva and urine kit based on your symptoms and schedule. The best way to test cortisol and DHEA is through saliva; neurotransmitters like serotonin and dopamine are best tested in urine.

Blood testing is only helpful for DHEA-S. Cortisol is best tested at least two to four times during the day and night by saliva or urine. Most doctors are familiar with two adrenal diseases—1) Addison's disease (hypoadrenia) and 2) Cushing's (high cortisol) —and will only run additional tests for these if your symptoms are very severe. In most cases, these traditional blood tests will not help you determine if you are experiencing adrenal fatigue syndrome, so your physician may tell you you're fine, but you still don't feel well. I highly recommend that you get the right saliva and urine testing based on your symptoms.

Let me explain more about the two important adrenal hormones, DHEA and cortisol.

**DHEA** is dehydroepiandrosterone, an androgenic substance made in the adrenal cortex. A short-term (trauma) or long-term (constant little stressors) cause of severe imbalance—too much or too little—can cause problems. Aging (something we can't stop) also contributes to falling DHEA levels.

Symptoms of low DHEA levels include fatigue, exhaustion after exercise, changes in metabolism and body shape, depression, decreased sex drive, and poor memory. Symptoms of elevated levels are anxiety, panic attacks, heart palpitations, sleep disturbances, confusion, and salt cravings.

**Cortisol** is an adenocortical hormone. Stable cortisol levels are essential for life. Cortisol should be tested at least two times during the day, but four times is better. Ideally the saliva samples would be collected upon waking, around noon, between 4-5 p.m. and then between 10 p.m. and midnight. These testing times may be altered based on your normal work, awake, and nighttime schedules. Cortisol is supposed to be the highest in the morning to help wake you up and then goes down as nighttime progresses.

Low levels of cortisol affect the functioning of the body systems that control energy metabolism of all the nutrients: carbohydrates, proteins, and fat. Symptoms include fatigue, sometimes just in the morning and sometimes all day long, low blood pressure, and a lowered immune system.

Symptoms of high cortisol are insulin resistance/glycemic control due to disturbed carbohydrate metabolism, trouble falling asleep, disturbed sleep at night, irritability, anxiety, heart palpitations, and sugar cravings. Too much progestin and taking birth control pills can also elevate cortisol levels.

**Serotonin** is a hormone in the pineal gland that acts as a neurotransmitter (chemical messenger) and affects sleep, moods, appetite, learning, and the constriction of blood vessels. It is made from an amino acid (the breakdown of protein) called tryptophan. Low levels can contribute to depression, food cravings and a ravenous appetite, headaches, hot flashes, and sleep issues. High levels are usually caused by selective serotonin reuptake inhibitors (SSRI, antidepressant medications) and stress. Once serotonin is measured through urine testing, therapies such as 5-hydroxytryptophan (5-HTP), dosed according to the lab values (usually 100-300 mg/day), intense regular exercise, stress reduction, touch, comedy and laughter, eating moderate carbohydrates, limiting or omitting all alcohol, refined sugars, and caffeine, and, of course, balancing the other hormones will help get serotonin in check.

Some other neurotransmitters that can be helpful to test and adjust:

1) **Dopamine** is produced in many parts of the brain. In relation to weight and appetite, it is responsible for

satisfaction, and low levels increase addictive behavior and cravings.

2) **Epinephrine** is another excitatory neurotransmitter. When levels are low it can make weight loss difficult. Balanced epinephrine levels are also important for emotional stability. Mental balance is helpful when trying to eat healthier and limit emotional eating and binging.
3) γ**-Aminobutyric acid (GABA)** can contribute to sleep issues, therefore contributing to adrenal issues and affecting muscle tone. A good health practitioner will decide whether to test these after a thorough interview.

Okay, okay, so now some of you are thinking: I took my saliva test. I have ongoing fatigue. I've had a lot of stress over the last six months or as long as two years. What do I do about it?

Reducing stress, of course, is the key. You've probably heard some of these, but there are many simple things you can do that are good for body. Copy this list and keep it handy.

1) Practice stress reduction techniques such as Reiki, reflexology, breathing exercises, guided imagery, acupuncture, meditation, biofeedback, aromatherapy, cranial sacral massage therapy, stone massage therapy, yoga, tai chi…the list goes on. Choose anything that helps you relax and quiets your inner nervous system. The last chapter expands on a few of these modalities.
2) Get adequate sleep each night. This means uninterrupted sleep of at least six and preferably seven to ten hours per night. Inadequate sleep increases the hormones cortisol

and grehlin, which increases your appetite and can lead to a decrease in your self-control.

3) Get your hormones in balance. Assess all of your hormones. For men, tests should be done for testosterone and estradiol by saliva. Free testosterone by blood can also be helpful. For women, estradiol, estriol, progesterone, and testosterone should be assessed by saliva. Your practitioner may recommend bioidentical hormones, DHEA, or other over-the-counter supplements. But be sure to choose a high-quality brand, preferably through a licensed practitioner. Please do not take DHEA without testing your DHEA levels as well as testosterone levels. When you increase DHEA in a woman, testosterone also goes up, often causing irritability, a lower libido, and just a nasty attitude. This could be great or bad, depending on your body's needs.
4) Exercise! Any exercise three to seven days a week for at least fifteen minutes to get you started. Strength train, watch a DVD, or walk. Anything form of physical activity for the first three weeks is critical in establishing a new habit. You might want to purchase a pedometer and try to add two thousand steps a day until you get to at least ten thousand steps per day. ANYTHING!
5) Clean up your diet. Eat a lot of fresh raw vegetables and fruits. You may have to limit your total fruit servings to two to three servings per day depending on your insulin, cortisol, and body fat levels. Your health practitioner or dietitian can guide you. Get at least 20% or more of your calories from lean animal or plant proteins. Eat foods with a lower glycemic index. *Avoid* refined foods, especially sugar, trans fatty acids, and fried foods. Drink filtered water.

6) Add nutritional support through supplements. Red blood cells take about three to four months to turn over, and your DNA takes six to twelve months or longer, so be patient for results. You don't feel your cholesterol going up or cancer forming. It often takes many years. You rarely feel prevention, either, so just do it!! Add a whole food supplement that is supported with medical studies, such as Juice Plus and Vineyard Blend by NSA, fish oil, and vitamin D3. The next chapter goes into these foundational nutritional supplements in more detail. You may need to consider taking herbs, tonic herbs, and especially adatogens to help with adrenal issues. Some examples are eleuthro, Rhodiola rosea, Schisandra, Astragalus, Cordyceps, or Reishi. If your practitioner or you think that you also have mineral imbalances, then you will want to take a sample of hair for a hair mineral tissue test. You may need to add individual mineral supplements such as magnesium at nighttime, but again rely on hair or blood individualized testing before using individual vitamins or minerals. Magnesium may help with sugar cravings, PMS, anxiety, and muscle cramping, or you may need to take it due to a depletion caused by taking blood pressure prescription medication.
7) Eliminate any allergens. Keep a food diary and do food challenges with the help of a dietitian or health-care practitioner.
8) Reduce or preferably omit all alcohol and caffeine for three to twelve months. Of course, if you are drinking as much as four cups of fancy coffee a day or two Cokes every day, start reducing by one to two servings every week, so you aren't miserable and don't have headaches.

**Summary:**

If you have been experiencing fatigue and high amounts of stress without a diagnosis or improvement through traditional medicine, test your cortisol and DHEA levels by a saliva test and serotonin by urine and maybe a few other neurotransmitters. You can also bring James L. Wilson's book, *Adrenal Fatigue, the 21st Century Stress Syndrome*, to your health care practitioner or doctor if he or she can't help you with your symptoms. Life is too wonderful to be tired all the time. Get support and don't give up!

"The world belongs to the energetic." Ralph Waldo Emerson

**Additional Resources:**

Nutrition, Connection, Balance, 1443 W. Schaumburg Rd., Ste. 22, Schaumburg, Illinois, 60194, 847-985-1200
www.nutritionconnectionbalance.com
www.vearlytakesjuiceplus.com
*Adrenal Fatigue, the 21st Century Stress Syndrome*, James L. Wilson
www.adrenalfatigue.org
*The UltraMind Solution*, Mark Hyman, M.D.
*Safe Uses of Cortisol*, William Jeffries

# CHAPTER SEVEN: Nutritional Support

Nutrigenomics is the study of phytochemicals or isoflavones and how they interfer with the RNA and DNA (the building blocks of your genes) in the body. The good news is that you can have a new body in six to twelve months if you clean up your eating and drinking and balance your hormones, neurotransmitters, and get active!

Does nutrition really matter? You bet! Many doctors, families, and other Americans eat Pop-Tarts for breakfast, fast food for lunch, frozen dinners, and soda, sugared teas, and coffee all day and can't figure out why they have allergies, headaches, depression, and obesity. Wake up! Food can be bad or good medicine! *Hippocrates long ago said, "Let food be thy medicine, and medicine be thy food."* Hippocrates also said, "Natural forces within us are the true healers of disease"—and he lived between 460 B.C. and approximately 400 B.C. What a wise man!

I encourage you not to be one of the patients who come to me perplexed about why they got breast cancer, heart disease, or osteoporosis. It is so much easier and cheaper to prevent disease. I say, pay now or pay *big* later! The problem is you don't always feel prevention coming on or believe that it is valuable. Also, there are no guarantees. I believe we all have our own life lessons and challenges from which we learn and grow, and karma and external stress that we can't always control. Let's start with some facts that hopefully will motivate you and help you realize you are what you eat and drink.

- The risks for cancer, diabetes, heart disease, and death increase as your weight rises.
- More gallbladder issues, hypertension, and colon cancer occur from being overweight.
- Cancer has surpassed heart disease as the leading cause of death for those under age eighty-five, according to some agencies.
- Forty-seven percent of heart attack victims die on the spot.
- Inflammatory disease has increased by 50% in Americans.
- This generation of young people is expected to have a shorter lifespan than their parents, according to Dr. David Katz at Yale University.
- Drink plenty of water, because water has so many functions in the body and the human body can't store water. Water is a part of every cell. Water regulates body temperature and carries nutrients, oxygen, and glucose to cells and organs. It removes waste from the body and keeps stools softer.
- Water is the most essential and abundant component in the human body. It's 60% of body weight for young adults and 50% of body weight for the elderly. The more muscle you have, the more water you have (and need), sometimes comprising 65%-75% of your body!
- Drink filtered water and avoid bottled water in plastic as much as possible. Bottled water may not be cleaner than

tap water anyway. Plastic leaks xenoestrogens, which have been associated with cancer.

- More than one-third of all older adults have inadequate water consumption (National Health and Nutrition Examination Survey, 1999-2000).
- Dietary supplements are very safe. There have been fewer than five deaths per year over the last twenty years attributed to supplements.
- Thirty thousand or more people die every year from food poisoning and over-the-counter pain relievers.
- About one hundred forty thousand deaths or more occur per year from properly dosed prescription drugs.

What should you eat? The bulk of your daily diet should be lots of raw vegetables and fruits. However, if you are diabetic or insulin resistant, limit your consumption of fruits. Also eat adequate protein and good fats. Do I sound like a broken record?

Why eat vegetables? Here are a few very important reasons:

- **Indole-3-carbinol (I3C)** and **Di-indole-methane (DIM)** are found in cruciferous vegetables such as cabbage, kale, broccoli. They block the effects of excessive estrogen and improve testosterone and estrogen metabolism.
- **Calcium D-Glucarate (CDG)** helps the process of glucuronidation (how the body rids itself of toxins). It is also found in fruits and vegetables, but usually not in large amounts. The best sources are alfalfa sprouts, apples, apricots, broccoli, brussels sprouts, grapefruit, and cherries.

**What base supplements (foundation) should you take?**

- **Whole food supplement**. My first recommendation is Juice Plus and Vineyard Blend by NSA, since they are whole food concentrates in a capsule or chewable form and have peer-reviewed medical studies in humans. Juice Plus is rich in vitamins, minerals, antioxidants, and other phytonutrients from the juice powders from seven different fruits (Orchard Blend) and the juice powders from eight different vegetables and two grains (Garden Blend). The Vineyard Blend has eight varieties of berries, the Concord grape, coenzyme Q10 and additional ingredients that protect the brain, heart, and organs affected by oxidative stress, and the circulatory system. Between 2002 and 2004, I gave my hormone patients a choice between taking a good multiple vitamin/mineral supplement or Juice Plus and Vineyard Blend. The patients with the best hormone balance and overall health markers were the patients taking Juice Plus and Vineyard Blend. The Juice Plus and Vineyard Blend help bridge the gap between what we are doing (not enough fruits and vegetables) and what we should be doing (eating 9-13 servings of raw, tree-ripened fruits and vegetables/day). Taking the Juice Plus and Vineyard Blend is like body insurance.
- **Vitamin D.** Vitamin D works more like a hormone than a vitamin. It has a protective influence over diabetes, muscle maintenance, depression, seasonal affective disorder (SAD), heart-related issues, all the autoimmune diseases like lupus, Crohn's, and MS, and, of course, bone health, such as osteoporosis. Since I work with so many men and women with hormone issues and osteopenia, the beginning of weakening bones, I have been asking all

my patients to ask their gynecologist, health practitioner, or physician to test their blood levels of 25-hydroxy vitamin D3 levels. Once you have your blood test results, I aim for the values of 25 hydroxy vitamin D3 to be at least 50-100 without any of the conditions listed above and 75-100 or more if you already have osteoporosis or autoimmune disease. If you are one of those people like me that need 5,000 IU of vitamin D3 to keep levels within ideal, it is important to test your blood calcium levels at least three to four months after going on a higher dose of vitamin D3. A serum calcium is usually in a normal complete blood count (CBC) that your doctor orders once a year. I strongly encourage a blood test to get the right amount of D3 for your individual and unique body; however, if you just had a doctor's visit or you don't have health insurance, I recommend that you can take 1,000-2,000 IU of cholecalciferol (D3). I do not recommend higher doses without testing. Please do not use ergocalciferol, (D2) and check your multiple vitamins (which I do not recommend) and your calcium supplement for the right form of vitamin D3 (cholecalciferol).

We used to think that being in the sunlight regularly was enough to get adequate vitamin D levels. However, based on my testing, as well as the clinical evidence, this is not true. There is not a good natural way to get enough vitamin D3 without supplementation. The American Dietetic Association as well as researchers and experts such as Dr. Bruce Hollis recommends taking vitamin D3 supplements. There are other ways to take in vitamin D3 but there are disadvantages. One way is to be in a warm climate all year round and get sun, which is ill advised because of the risk of skin cancer. Another way is milk. Milk contains low levels of vitamin D. I'm not a milk fan and have never given my children milk. Milk can promote food sensitivities, sinus inflammations, eczema, and allergies as well as headaches in about 49% of people in my clinical experience. And finally, cod liver oil is another source of D3, but daily compliance is usually poor. There is concern about the amount of Vitamin of A in some bottles as well as the inconsistent serum levels that I get when testing people taking cod liver oil.

**In summary**: get your blood levels of 25-hydroxy vitamin D3 levels assessed if possible, check any supplements you are taking to ensure the right form of vitamin D3 (cholecalciferol), but remember the "general or mixed supplement" usually will not contain the 1,000-2,000 or more IU of D3 that you will need. I have seen some incredible improvements and management in my clients' hormone functioning, such as thyroid and neurotransmitter functioning such as serotonin levels, as well as mood, bone density, muscle retention, and symptoms associated with autoimmune diseases, when patients reach and maintain the optimal levels of D3.

**Fish oil.** Omega-3s are used to reduce inflammation; to prevent weight gain, insulin resistance, osteoporosis, arthritis, lupus, and cardiovascular disease; and to help with cognitive functioning and moods. Omega-3 fatty acids (fish oil) contain eicosapentaenoic acid (EPA) and docosahexaenoic acid (DHA). Both EPA and DHA affect your gene expression (what diseases could get turned on) and are important for just about all health therapies. EPA and DHA can block inflammatory markers (series 2 prostaglandins). I recommend fish oil capsules or oil. There are many pure brands, but I gravitate towards Nordic Naturals because most people tolerate it and the company guarantees low mercury, PCBs, and contaminants. In addition, the company makes many combinations that can be matched to each individual's personal need. Without any formal testing, I recommend you get 1,000-1,200 mg of EPA and DHA combined. Higher doses may be needed with testing and certain medical conditions such as high triglycerides or arthritis. There's also prescription fish oil, called Lovaza, that has 465 mg of EPA and 375 mg of DHA per capsule. Ask your health practitioner for guidance.

- I also recommend you sprinkle ground flax seed on your food and in your shakes and salads, but not in place of fish oil, in addition to it! The alpha linolenic acid in flax requires adequate enzymes to convert to EPA and DHA. These enzymes can be reduced by stress, insulin resistance, and prescription medications. So it is best to see a health professional for appropriate dosing and individualized ratios of EPA to DHA for your individual needs.
- Other possible base supplements such as calcium, magnesium, and B12 may be needed, but only if you have a deficiency created by poor food intake, a disease, or prescription depletion.
- **Calcium.** I prefer getting calcium from whole foods, green vegetables, and shakes, and recommend getting the best form, calcium citrate, if you are just achieving your daily calcium through a tablet or capsule. If you are getting your calcium through a shake or a high quality mixed calcium supplement, it may be all right to have other calcium salts, such as carbonate, etc. Try to achieve

about 1,000 mg per day of calcium from your food and shake sources. A very important fact to know is that as you lose weight, calcium excretion increases and calcium absorption is decreased. Women have a 100% risk of bone fractures as they lose weight if they do not get adequate protein and do not lift weights—another reason to strength train and get enough protein, as I have described in an earlier chapter. Some food sources to help you get started are:

- Dairy Products: 1 cup, 100-500 mg
- Leafy greens (kale, bok choy, spinach): ½ cup, 80-130 mg
- Beans (black and navy): 1 cup, 120-130 mg
- Fortified cereals: 1 cup, 40-300 mg
- Fortified rice milk, soy milk, and almond milk: 1 cup, 250-400 mg
- **B12.** B12 helps form blood and helps in metabolism and energy production. But only supplement if you need B12 after a blood or cellular test to get your values to ideal levels. Again, every vitamin has rule. I want to give you an example why you may want to test first: a study in the November 18, 2009, issue of the *Journal of the American Medical Association* (*JAMA*) showed supplementation with high folic acid (800 mcg) and B12 (400 mcg) increased lung cancer risk. Now these 6,837 patients had ischemic heart disease. But I can give you many examples of these kinds of studies; plus, don't most people these days have some medical issue or take a prescription medication? Yes, unfortunately.
- **Magnesium.** Magnesium is a wonderful cofactor in bone formation and other nerve and muscle conduction. Some medications, such as blood pressure medications, lower magnesium. Test by serum testing or a hair

analysis. The blood test is just fine if you are looking for a prescription related depletion, but if you are looking for people with symptoms of anxiety, ADHD, restless leg syndrome, and athletes, then I recommend a hair analysis.

**Weight loss supplements**...fat burners? Conjugated linoleic acid (CLA), niacin, fiber, caffeine, curcumin, garcinia (hydroxy citric acid, HCA), coleus forskohlii, etc., all have some thermogenic, stimulant affect or fat loss studies to support them, but so little benefit compared to eating right, balancing your hormones, and exercising. If you want to take one of these supplements, rely on your licensed health professional, not a health store salesman. Make sure the ingredients do not interact with any prescription medications you are taking and do not interfere with any of your hormone or neurotransmitter levels or therapies. I often use whole food shakes like Complete Shake, whey protein, or medical foods like Ultra Meal Plus by Metagenics.

## Alkalinity and Acidity

Clinically, the discussion around alkalinity and acidity (pH) is a controversial topic. Most people and professionals believe that if your body is in a state of acidity you will have a hard time losing weight or body fat and have a higher incidence of disease.

The pH scale ranges from 0-14. Neutral is 7, acidic levels are below 7, and 8 to 14 is alkaline. Water has a pH of 7 and cola is acidic at 2.8. You want to avoid extremes in the body so that you have balance and a more alkaline or neutral pH. This can be assessed by pH strips. The body needs to stay within a normal pH of about 7.35 to 7.45 in the blood stream.

Urine and saliva test strips can assess pH levels at home. When you have acidic saliva or urine, it can indicate that you are leaching necessary minerals from your system, including calcium. Any mineral leached from the body can contribute to conditions such as osteoporosis, tooth decay, kidney stones, elevated lipid levels, and stress.

Stress also contributes to increasing body fat and weight issues. Stress of any kind elevates cortisol, disrupts sleep, increases your appetite and cravings for carbohydrates, and increases weight gain and insulin resistance. Chapter six is a good chapter to review regarding the adrenals and treatment for "stress."

So what can you eat to help alkaline your body? Think green. Add dark green, leafy vegetables such as spinach, kale, broccoli, and Swiss chard. Most people do not consume enough of these foods. By consuming more of these vegetables, your system will naturally become more alkaline, probably go through a natural detox, and be less stressed.

Interestingly, the heart chakra, which is an energy center in the body, is green. This chakra signifies harmony and balance. This is the state that we want in the body. The key here is that most people do not eat enough vegetables, so the majority of people are acidic. Again, the way to adjust this imbalance is to eat more dark green, leafy vegetables and avoid sugar-filled and processed foods. I will not be providing you with a list of alkaline and acid producing foods because, other than dark green vegetables, there is disagreement on what foods are acid forming and what foods are alkaline forming in the body.

One of my closest friends, Kathleen Stefancin, is a raw food advocate and a registered dietitian. She makes some of the best raw food salads and green smoothies I've ever eaten. She's allowed me to include three of her favorite fruit and vegetable smoothie recipes in this book so that others can also enjoy them. Thanks Kathleen! When making green smoothies, be sure to buy as many organic fruits and vegetables as you can afford.

**Spinach Sequence** by Kathleen Stefancin of Smartpicks
1 red apple (cut out the core)
1 banana (peeled)
2 big handfuls of organic spinach
1 sliver of ginger the size of a quarter (optional)
1 teaspoon ground flax seed
Pinch of kelp (I use Spice Garden Glandular Kelp)
Water

Puree in a blender. Makes 2 cups.

**Dandelion Desire by** Kathleen Stefancin of Smartpicks
1 brown pear (cut out the core)
1 red apple (cut out the core)
1 stalk of celery
½ bunch dandelion greens
Water

Puree in a blender.

**Romaine Romance** by Kathleen Stefancin of Smartpicks
1 banana (peeled)
1 red apple (cut out the core)
2 cups romaine lettuce
Sliver of ginger the size of a quarter (optional)
Water

Puree in a blender.

If you are nervous about trying these recipes, my favorite lazy and/or picky person's blended salad is what I call Go Bananas or my Mango Sunrise.

**Go Bananas** by Valerie Early of NCB
½ banana (peeled)
½ Granny Smith apple, peeled or unpeeled (cut out the core)
2 cups of baby spinach
Water

**Mango Sunrise** by Valerie Early of NCB
1 mango, peeled
3-4 fresh or frozen strawberries
1 cup of spinach
1 cup of romaine lettuce
1 big leaf of kale
Water

**Instructions for green smoothies**: In a blender, put in enough water to cover the blade. Next add the fruits and blend, then add the green leafy vegetables and blend again. Finally add any other ingredients such as the ginger and blend one more time. You can add more water as needed for desired consistency.

**Summary:**

Avoid an acidic state by eating more dark green vegetables to prevent imbalances and stress in the body that contribute to body fat.

**Additional Resources:**

For additional green smoothie recipes go to: www.smart-picks.com
*The China Study*, T. Colin Campbell, Ph.D.
*The Biology of Belief*, Bruce H. Lipton, Ph.D.
*Eating in the Light…Making the Switch to Vegetarianism*, Doreen Virtue, Ph.D., and Becky Prelitz
*Volumetrics Weight-Control Plan*, Barbara Rolls, Ph.D., and Robert Barnett
*Best Life Diet*, Robert Greene
*Fast Food Nation*, Eric Schlosser
*Thin for Life*, Anne Fletcher, MS, R.D.
*The Way to Eat*, David Katz, M. D., MPH, and Maura Gonazalez, MS, R.D.

# CHAPTER EIGHT: Vibrational Alignment

Are you in vibrational alignment with yourself, your feelings, and your life purpose? Do you feel happy and passionate about your life on a daily basis? When do you feel this way? All day, at work, or only on the weekends? For many people, only vacations provide happiness and relief from "daily life." When you feel joy and peace, you will experience supreme health and balance. Two of my favorite authors, Esther and Jerry Hicks, through the teachings of Abraham, sum it up so clearly by saying that no matter what you are exposed to—germs, poor water quality, a lower energy field (negativity) of another person—if you are in a highly aligned vibration with yourself and are feeling good, the exposure to these influences, whether physical, emotional, or energetic, will not make you ill. Isn't it wonderful to know that you have the control of your health and well-being? The escrow of everything you have ever wanted is just waiting, but you must realize that it exists and then snatch it up. When I ask a patient, "Are you happy?" more than 75% cry on the spot; even the men squirm in their chair, get glassy eyed, and start looking up, repeating a dream they have or had but aren't fulfilling. Why? They have jobs that they are supposed to do since they have a degree or skill to match and bills to pay. But, interestingly enough, since most of my services are paid out of pocket, 80% of my clients have the house, money, and family they desire but are not living passionately and doing the daily activities that make them feel pure bliss. Rediscover your dream and start living it; improved health and energy will follow! Did you want to be a musician, make a difference in the world, and help animals? What is your dream?

Here's an example that may help you realize that it is your daily life that makes you ill, not something else. When you are getting ready to go on vacation and have to get up at 5 a.m. to catch a plane, do you feel tired or depressed that you have to get up? Does it feel different than a work morning? Yes! Sometimes you even wake a few times at night, waiting for that alarm to go off, but there isn't any agitation, dread, or fatigue if you are leaving for a trip. For kids, watch how they act on a school morning versus a Saturday or Sunday morning. My final example is libido...the sex drive. I have many men and women that are not feeling the spark physically or mentally, but when they are on vacation they have no problem experiencing intimacy and orgasms on a daily basis. Now what changed? Their hormones, an illness magically went away, or their environment? Less stress and fewer chores with additional sunshine and happiness usually occur on a vacation. Need I say more? Re-evaluate. Last year my eleven-year old-son, Dillon, said that he hated Mondays. I said, "Me, too, so what can we do about it?" I'm always saying, if you don't like something, change it! I decided to stop seeing patients on Mondays and be home when my kids got home from school. This change has made a world of difference to me and my children.

What happens if you are a far cry from finding and living your passion? First, awareness is important, then I recommend some good reading, journaling, some good talks with friends that you have had for a while, creating a dream board, and even getting some counseling or life coaching if needed or desired. Some reading resources are listed at the end of this chapter. Creating a dream board is easy. Just look through magazines or go onto the Internet and think about all the things that you would like to have, places you want to go, events and people that invoke joy within you, and place photos on that dream board that make you smile and bring you bliss. The next step is finding a way to settle things down in your body: quiet the mind, balance the nervous system and all your organs, and reconnect to your own energy. Everything in life comes down to energy. Some wonderful tools I highly recommend are Reiki, guided imagery, acupuncture, journeying, meditation, martial arts, and biofeedback. I will elaborate on the first two modalities.

My favorite energy tool is called the Reiki. I became a Reiki Master in 2003 so that I could teach Reiki to my own children, my patients, and friends, and use it on my lovely dog, Lightening. I use it daily on my own body and on inanimate objects like my patient files, lab test results, house, and dream board. Reiki is one of the few healing modalities that can be learned at any age and can instantly change your vibration with an attunement or treatments. I feel that we often give our own power and healing ability away to other people: doctors, health practitioners, and even family. Once you have an attunement you can use Reiki on yourself and on others...without continual visits or expense. Reiki is a hands-on healing founded in Japan. Reiki is a technique that is administered through gentle touch. Reiki transfers to a person during an attunement given by a Reiki Master. An attunement is a process that balances the body and chakras (energy centers in the body), changes auras, and has potential for healing the physical body by creating an unlimited channel of energy that allows an individual to tap into his or her own life force energy. Once Reiki is received, it can be used to enhance self-healing, create feelings of relaxation and peace, and relieve aches and pains.

Reiki is a biofield therapy classification, according to the National Institutes of Health Center for Complementary and Alternative Medicine (NCCAM). Biofield modalities affect the body's energy fields through touch and/or specific hand positions on or around the body. Reiki is used in many clinical environments, such as emergency rooms, hospitals, and psychiatric wards. It is being used for many conditions and symptoms, like cancer, fatigue syndromes, stress, immune dysfunctions, and delivering a baby! My life, as well as the lives of many of my students and friends, has been changed after obtaining Reiki. There continue to be more and more clinical studies on Reiki. Here is a list to give you an idea of the various benefits.

**There are physical benefits:**

- Improves the immune system
- Reduces blood pressure and the heart rate
- Used in HIV patients
  - o Philadelphia researchers
  - o Reduces pain and anxiety (after 20 minutes)
- Diabetes

- o University of Michigan
  - ▪ Reduces Cardiovascular disease, pain, and neuropathy
- o Reduced insulin

**It helps with various cancer issues:**

- Chemotherapy and radiation side effects
- Less pain in advanced cancer patients
  - o *Journal of Pain and Symptom Management,* November 2003
  - o Integrative Therapies for Children with Cancer, Columbia Presbyterian Medical Center, New York, New York, is using it with various treatment and training.
- Hospice

**NIH's Warren Grant Magnuson Clinical Center, Bethesda, Maryland:**

- Provided medical care for all patients participating in NIH research protocols
- 7,000 patients per year
- 68,000 outpatients per year
- Two Reiki Masters train the staff, patients' families, and give treatments.
  - o Screaming patients in pain have improvements in pain after five to ten minutes of Reiki.
    - ▪ Patients have a change in attitude: improved outlook.

**Other medical studies:**

- University of Washington—fibromyalgia
- University of Michigan—neuropathy and cardiovascular factors in diabetics
- Temple University—Advanced AIDS, quality of life
- Cleveland Clinic—Anxiety and disease progression in prostate cancer

**Reiki helps with mental issues:**

- mental health
- addictions
- smoking
- overeating
- depression—six weeks less hopelessness
- "According to *Alternative Therapies in Health and Medicine* (May/June 2004), Reiki gives energy and balances the body, relaxes, balances the energy centers (chakras) of the body, and soothes trauma, anxiety, and panic attacks."

Reiki is a wonderful way to help you enhance your own energy, healing, and life. I strongly encourage you to take a Reiki training class or schedule a Reiki session today to bring your body and life back into balance! Here are a few statements written by clients that have taken my Reiki classes and are now Reiki Masters:

"Reiki is one of those things that affect you in ways you don't even realize until later on—you look back and discover that some profound changes have occurred in your life after being exposed to it. The momentum you can build for yourself when you are on purpose and in balance is really amazing! I am able to clearly see the benefit that Reiki brings to people. When someone tells me that they have been fibromyalgia pain free for an entire week after receiving Reiki—and all the things they were able to accomplish and participate in that they otherwise wouldn't have felt up to—I am so thankful that we have this in our world to share." Elizabeth Kemper, March 26, 2010

"Reiki has been a transformational experience for me. Since becoming a Reiki Master I look at life in a different way; I see more of the good in the world." Joe Cirincione, March 26, 2010

"Becoming a Reiki Master has brought a new level of awareness of how positive and negative vibrations (energy) affect our daily lives. It has given me a clearer understanding of how choosing positive energy, people, and surroundings help us to stay in our vibrational alignment. Reiki has given me much peace and happiness and the ability to share it with others." Sherry Panico, March 28, 2010.

Guided imagery is probably my second favorite integrated therapy because it's an audio CD that has words with music. It's affordable, doesn't require a lot of extra time, and can really change the brain's messages to the rest of your body. Belleruth Naparstak has some amazing audio CDs to help you reduce stress, lose weight, sleep better, recover from surgery faster, and affirm your own greatness. When a client even refuses to listen to an audio CD at bedtime, it's a red flag for healing resistance. An audio CD costs around $20, doesn't require that you carve out extra time from your day, and doesn't require a belief or deep understanding of how it works. I recommend that my patients listen to a CD every night at bedtime for at least two to six months straight. The CDs are also great for downloading onto an iPod and using while traveling, especially when you are in an airplane or in a noisy hotel or city.

I want to expose you to the fourth energy center (chakra) in your body. It is the heart. The color green represents this chakra. We now know that the heart rules the body, more so than the brain. What foods have the highest vibration and green color? Plant foods, especially leafy green vegetables. It's so easy to see all the connections to good health, whether you are studying energy, plant foods, or the body. We just need to pay attention and listen!

Lastly, one must be in personal vibrational balance, eating healthy, exercising, and balancing one's hormones, adrenals, neurotransmitters, and anything else out of whack! Do not forget to look at behavior and food habits. It's wise to really examine why you overeat or choose unhealthy choices that do not benefit you in the long run. The answer is usually a combination of events: tradition, rewarding oneself, feelings, memories, going too long in between eating, poor sleep, low nutrition quality, and hormone imbalances. Pay attention to your feelings. Are you mad, sad, or glad when you eat? Were you rewarded with food as a child? As a child, sweets were definitely intertwined with love at our house. Do you have a common trigger to overeating: stress, loneliness, a TV commercial, a smell, skipping meals, your company, eating out, or traveling?

Most bad habits become a chain of events. For example, a patient that had lost over thirty pounds over a six-month period, and then proceeded to go on vacation, correlated going on vacation to gaining weight. While away, she exercised daily, walked miles, ate lots of healthy foods, and limited her alcoholic beverages. She came back a few more pounds lighter. However, a month later she came in and had gained five pounds. She said, "That darned vacation!" I noted that it wasn't the vacation, but that after she returned home, she did not get groceries right away, ate out for most lunches, got caught up with work, and avoided the gym for the first two weeks after returning from her vacation. What actually caused the weight gain was not returning immediately to a healthy lifestyle, rather than the vacation itself. So, it is helpful to know the real facts and the triggers so your analysis of weight gain is accurate. It may not be the vacations or another positive event that caused you to lose your balance. Journal after you eat something you wish you hadn't. What was the feeling or reason that you overindulged? It doesn't take long to see the triggers if you are honest and stay aware; however, you must also be willing to change. Getting a registered dietitian, a counselor, a life coach or a psychologist, or even a health buddy can be very helpful. Having a person to be accountable to and someone that can be objective and supportive can be a relief so you can move past old unhealthy habits!

**Summary**:

Get excited about your life; align your vibration to your passion and dreams, while keeping an open mind to other "energy" and "healing" modalities to help you achieve your body and health goals.

The quote that seems to sum it up for me—and hopefully will help you—is: *"The doctor of the future will give no medicine, but will interest his patients in the care of the human frame, in diet and in the cause and prevention of disease." —Thomas A. Edison*

**Resources:**

*Ask and It Is Given,* Esther and Jerry Hicks
*The Law of Attraction*, Esther and Jerry Hicks
*The Spirit of Reiki,* by William Lee Rand, Walter Lubeck, and Arjava Petter
*The Original Reiki Handbook of Dr. Makio Usui*, by Frank Arjava Petter
*The Secret*, Rhonda Byrne
*Mending the Past and Healing the Future with Soul Retrieval,* Alberto Villoldo, Ph.D.
*Excuses Begone!* Dr. Wayne W. Dyer
*Defying Gravity,* Carolyn Myss
*Spiritual Nutrition*, Gabriel Cousens
*Love, Medicine & Miracles,* Bernie Siegel, M.D.
*The Power of the Your Subconscious*, Joseph Murphy, Ph.D., D.D.
*Breaking the Food Seduction*, Dr. Neal Bernard
*Potatoes not Prozac*, Kathleen DesMaisons
www.reiki.org

You are a beautiful human being. Remember, your body works like a system; your arm is not in one corner, your brain in another corner, and your uterus in another. Plant foods have amazing life force energy, nutrients, vitamins, minerals, and thousands of phytochemicals that work with your body's system.

It's really so simple…follow the *Eight Ways to Lose your Blubber*:

1) monitor your calories,
2) eat the right carbohydrates, protein and fat grams for your body,
3) be active and maintain an optimal body fat level,
4) maintain healthy thyroid, insulin and glucose levels,
5) assess and balance your hormones,
6) properly measure your adrenals and neurotransmitter levels,
7) obtain the right nutrition support through food, whole food supplementation, omega 3 fatty acids, vitamin D3 and other short term nutrients if needed and
8) love, balance and empower yourself, find your faith, embrace your relationships, live every minute with passion, be present and experience your highest vibrational alignment.

When you do these eight things, you will be a brilliant, happy, healthy person.

Made in the USA
Charleston, SC
18 October 2010